PUFFIN BOOKS

DRAGON IN THE HARBOUR

R. Dragon is back in the swim – in Weymouth harbour to be exact – after an unaccountable hibernation of nearly twenty years! While the local sailors and fishermen find nothing strange about such a creature approaching them face to face, many of the holiday-makers are more than a little disconcerted when they bump into him. But, as his admirers will know, R. Dragon is really very friendly and he decided hundreds of years ago that eating people is wrong. Now he only puts his teeth into his mouth when he wants to look especially smart or eat something really tasty.

However, despite his peaceful nature, life is not always easy for R. Dragon. Grumpy Colonel Ocklestone is moored nearby and there's nothing he likes more than complaining. And what about the mysterious goings-on aboard the *Money-Spider*? Fancying the idea of himself as a second Sherlock Holmes, R. Dragon sets out to discover what the two occupants of this boat are up to.

Adventure, excitement and fun lurk round every corner. R. Dragon enjoys himself enormously and so should young readers. Three other books about R. Dragon are available in Puffin: *Dragon in Danger*, *The Dragon's Quest* and *Green Smoke*.

Rosemary Manning was born in Dorset in 1911. After taking a Classics Degree, she has had a varied career in business, teaching, lecturing, and writing. In addition to five children's books, she has written several novels for adults and a number of short stories.

Rosemary Manning

Dragon in the Harbour

ILLUSTRATED BY
Peter Rush

PUFFIN BOOKS

PUFFIN BOOKS

Published by the Penguin Group
Penguin Books Ltd, 27 Wrights Lane, London W8 5TZ, England
Penguin Books USA Inc., 375 Hudson Street, New York, New York 10014, USA
Penguin Books Australia Ltd, Ringwood, Victoria, Australia
Penguin Books Canada Ltd, 10 Alcorn Avenue, Toronto, Ontario, Canada M4V 3B2
Penguin Books (NZ) Ltd, 182–190 Wairau Road, Auckland 10, New Zealand

Penguin Books Ltd, Registered Offices: Harmondsworth, Middlesex, England

First published by Kestrel Books 1980
Published in Puffin Books 1982
5 7 9 10 8 6

Printed in England by Clays Ltd, St Ives plc

For my friends, young and old.

In the words of the dragon:
May the garland of friendship ever be green!

Acknowledgements

We wish to thank the Marquess of Bath for his kind permission to use Longleat House, Wiltshire, as the place where the dragon's Aunt Dracula works on her book.

Thanks are also due to Captain H. E. Holden, D.S.C., Harbour-Master of Weymouth, for his helpful advice on harbour bye-laws and other nautical matters.

Contents

I

No Peace for a Dragon

THE dragon floated peacefully on the calm waters of Weymouth harbour, his eyes closed in sleep. He was very tired. He had arrived only the night before, after several days of hard sailing up the Channel from the West Country. It was now about nine o'clock in the morning, and the sun was just beginning to warm the tips of his yellow horns and fins, when his peace was rudely disturbed. He felt something sharp nudging his ribs, opened one eye and saw that it was the bows of a small motor-launch. A man in a peaked cap was steering it. Rather brusquely, this fellow asked the one eye he could see: 'Just what are you doing here?'

'Well, I *was* sleeping,' replied the dragon, crossly.

'I dare say. I'm asking you what you mean by mooring yourself here, right in the middle of Weymouth harbour. We didn't build this harbour for dragons, you know.'

'I am NOT moored,' said the dragon, and yawned hugely. A trickle of green smoke rose into the air. The man in the peaked cap was not impressed or even interested.

'I am Harbour-Master here,' he said.

'Charmed to meet you,' murmured the dragon, rather absently, closing the one eye that he'd opened.

'I repeat – you can't moor right in the middle like this,' said Peaked Cap.

With a weary gesture the dragon waved one paw backwards towards his tail fins. 'I've told you once – I am not moored,' he said. 'Anchored. That's what I am. *Anchored.*

Let's get our nautical terms right, shall we? You can see the anchor-chain if you care to look.'

The Harbour-Master pushed his launch along the dragon's side until he came to a heavy chain. It was neatly hooked over a pointed fin, with the slack coiled in an expert and seamanlike manner and slung over another fin.

'Yes, I see,' said the Harbour-Master. 'Tell me, just where did you get this chain and anchor?'

'It was lying around,' answered the dragon, carelessly. 'On a beach in Cornwall. Been there for I don't know how long. It was at least a hundred years ago that I found it.' The dragon's voice became dreamy. 'A lovely day in June, it was. I took it back to my cave, thinking it might be useful one day, and I was right.'

'Dragon!' cried the Harbour-Master in the loud tones of authority. 'Wake up and attend to me.'

'What is it now?' asked the dragon, in his most suffering voice. 'I am extremely tired, so make it short, please.'

'If you want to stay in the harbour, you can't anchor yourself in the middle or anywhere else. I'll give you a proper berth at the quay for twenty-four hours. How's that?'

'Fine!' answered the dragon, waking up properly.

'You'll have to observe the harbour bye-laws.'

'Give me a list of bye-laws and I'll observe 'em!' cried the dragon, adding a burst of song – a couple of lines from a sea-shanty: *'With my way-hey! Blow the man down!'*

'And you'll have to pay harbour dues, if you want to stay longer.'

'D'you mean money?' asked the dragon. 'Let's talk

about that after breakfast. Where can I get breakfast here, my good fellow?'

'I'm Mr Harbour-Master to you. There's a café along the quay,' answered Peaked Cap, pointing. 'I don't know if they keep any food for dragons.'

'No problem,' said the dragon. 'Just a dozen rolls with butter and marmalade will suit me, with a few fried eggs before that, and before *that*, a bowl of –'

'I can't stay here chatting,' interrupted the Harbour-Master. 'I've work to do. I'll send my Assistant along to fix you up with a berth.' He turned his launch about and went off up the harbour.

Now thoroughly awake, the dragon looked around him. He had not seen the harbour properly when he had sailed in, the night before. Weymouth was a working harbour, with a fishing fleet that berthed close to the Town Bridge. Further down the quay near the mouth of the harbour lay great ships with red funnels, that sailed to and from the Channel Isles of Guernsey and Jersey, carrying passengers, cars and lorries. And of course there were sailing boats of all kinds and sizes. Along the quays on each side stood houses, many of them with brightly-coloured front doors. Fitted in between the houses were pubs – the Jolly Sailor, the Cove, the Red Lion and many others, and there were tall warehouses, a fish-market and three or four restaurants and fish-and-chip shops.

After about ten minutes the dragon saw a man on the quay waving to him. The dragon waved back cheerfully, and then realized that it must be the Harbour-Master's Assistant, so he swam up to the quay, his wings folded and his legs tucked under him. The young man gave him a berth in an empty space near the Jolly Sailor inn. He was carrying a coil of rope, which he threw round a bollard and knotted with a twist of his hand. He then tossed the other end of the rope to the dragon, who caught it in one paw, looped it round one of his fins, and there he was, securely moored. Now it was more than time to think of breakfast. He didn't want to untie his mooring rope and clamber onto the quay, so he said, in an off hand way as though food was of little importance to him: 'I wonder if that café up there serves breakfast.'

'Breakfast? Oh, yes, Sir. You get very good breakfasts at the Mary-Rose Café.'

The dragon was pleased about that 'Sir'. Very right and proper, he thought. He gave a tremendous sigh that echoed across the harbour, and said in what he hoped was a rather faint voice: 'I really cannot climb up onto the quay. I'm exhausted. And anyway, I'm moored now.' He then paused and gazed hopefully at the Harbour-Master's Assistant. The young man, who wore a peaked cap like his superior officer's, was rather intrigued at having a dragon moored at the quay. This had never happened before in the seven years he'd worked in the Harbour-Master's office, so, feeling rather daring, he took a step nearer the dragon, and said:

'Would you like me to get you something, Sir?'

'That's a splendid idea!' exclaimed the dragon, brightening up at once. 'What are they likely to have? Buttered rolls? Fried eggs? Doughnuts? Apple fritters?'

'I'll find you something,' said the young man obligingly, and walked off towards the café. A few minutes later he returned with a large bag and a jug.

'There's coffee in the jug, Sir,' he explained.

'What's in the bag?' asked the dragon quickly. The coffee was less important.

'Well, Sir, there's a couple of custard tarts –'

'Delicious!'

'One doughnut –'

'Well, I suppose one's better than none,' observed the dragon in a disappointed tone.

'Three ham sandwiches –'

'With brown bread! How splendid!' interrupted the dragon.

'And there's two – no, *three* chocolate biscuits.'

'No fried eggs?' asked the dragon, anxiously.

'I couldn't have put them in a bag, you see, Sir,' explained the young man, 'and they wouldn't let me bring 'em to you on a plate.'

'Dear me! Whyever not? Were they afraid that I'd eat the plate?'

'Well, I don't rightly know, Sir, but they wouldn't let me have it.'

'Never mind,' said the dragon, picking up the doughnut and taking a large bite from it. 'My word! Am I hungry! This is a lovely doughnut. Full of jam. How much did you have to pay for all this, young man?'

'That's all right, Sir,' said the Harbour-Master's Assistant, adding with wild extravagance: 'The office will pay for it. We don't get a dragon in Weymouth harbour every week.'

The dragon looked up from the last piece of doughnut and thanked him politely.

'That young man will go far,' he said to himself, as the Harbour-Master's Assistant touched his peaked cap in a salute, and walked off down the quay. When he had finished the whole bagful of food and swallowed the coffee, the dragon screwed his litter into a ball, and being a tidy creature, he tossed it neatly into a litter-bin not far away on the quay.

Naturally, many people were most surprised and interested to see a dragon in the harbour, though not everyone seemed to know a dragon when they saw one, and he was amazed to hear himself referred to, several times, as 'some monster on a telly show, I shouldn't wonder'. He was most annoyed when someone prodded him with an umbrella to see if he was real. He blew a puff of green smoke at the woman who had prodded him. She had to be led away by her husband, coughing and choking, her eyes streaming with tears.

'Serve her right!' muttered the dragon, heartlessly.

At last he rolled over on his back, went to sleep and heard nothing more. He really did feel tired. It had taken him several days to reach Weymouth from his cave in Constantine Bay, on the north coast of Cornwall. First, he had flown overland to Plymouth and from there he sailed, or rather swam, to Weymouth. He had a dragonometer strapped round his right foreleg and this now registered 117 miles. It had been quite a trip.

Alas, he was not allowed to sleep for long. He was woken up after little more than half-an-hour by a snuffling in his left ear, followed by the words, in a shrill, childish voice: 'D'you know what the baby mouse said to the elephant?'

'I do not,' replied the dragon, crossly. 'Neither do I care. Go away, whoever you are. I am asleep.'

'You're not. You've woken up. *You* have to say: what did the baby mouse say to the elephant?'

The dragon sighed. 'All right,' he said. 'What *did* the baby mouse say?'

'You're mighty big!' shrieked the voice.

'Oh,' said the dragon. 'That seems to me a perfectly sensible remark. That baby mouse will go far, if you ask me.'

'No! NO!' cried the voice. 'The riddle isn't finished yet. You have to say: What did the elephant reply to the baby mouse?'

'Go to the top of the class, I should hope,' answered the dragon, still keeping his eyes tight shut.

'No, he didn't. He said: You're mighty small.'

'Not a very sparkling conversation,' observed the dragon.

15

'Ask what the mouse said then. Go on: ask what the mouse said.'

'I hope this isn't going on much longer, but all right. What did he say?'

'I know I'm mighty small. I ain't grown up yet!'

There was a long silence. Then the dragon opened his eyes and turned his head to see the owner of the voice. He found a small boy standing on the edge of the quay, close to his left ear, a boy with an upturned nose, bright blue eyes and a mop of fair hair which looked as if it could do with a brush. He was wearing a once-white T-shirt and faded blue jeans with patches on them.

'Coo! It's smashing having you here in the harbour!' exclaimed the boy. 'What's your name?'

'R. Dragon.'

'Mine's Adam.'

'Adam, do you live here?' asked the dragon, hoping that he didn't or there might be an endless stream of riddles every day.

'No, we're only here on holiday, worse luck. We're in a boarding-house along there.' He pointed up the quay towards the mouth of the harbour.

The dragon knew a boarding-house when he saw one, for there were many of them in Cornwall. You could generally tell them because there were bits of seaweed and bathing-costumes hanging out of windows, canvas shoes lying on window-sills, and downstairs, dining rooms with bottles of Tomato Ketchup and Daddy's Sauce standing on plastic table-tops and large potted ferns in the windows. The dragon ran his eye along the quay and spotted two or three such boarding-houses quite near him. He licked his lips with a green tongue. He was partial to Daddy's Sauce, which he had first met in Cornwall, when he found a bottle lying with some picnic rubbish. It had quite a lot of sauce left in it, and he found that it greatly improved his dinners of rather sandy prawns and fried fish and chips.

'Adam, could you do something for me?' asked the dragon.

'I expect so. What?'

'When the Daddy's Sauce is getting towards the bottom of the bottle, do you think you could – er – could just – er – whip it off the table and bring it to me?'

'Easy! 'Course I could! What'll you do for me, Dragon, if I bring you the Daddy's Sauce?'

'Listen to your riddles,' answered the dragon, closing his eyes.

'What else?'

'We'll see.'

'I'm afraid I ought to go,' said Adam.

'Ought you?' said the dragon, opening his eyes. 'It certainly seems a good idea. Visit me again, but not just yet.'

'I will, and I'll bring the sauce. And I'll bring my brother, too, maybe.'

'Oh, what brother is that?'

'MY brother. He's called John.'

'Does he ask riddles?'

'No, he's not interested in them.'

'Well, do bring him then.'

'Just before I go,' said Adam quickly, snorting a little down his nose, which was often stuffed up. 'How d'you help a deaf fisherman?'

'I don't know any deaf fishermen,' said the dragon.

'Oh, Dragon, you are hopeless. You have to ask me: how d'you help a deaf fisherman?'

'Suppose I don't particularly want to know the answer?'

'Well – oh, well – just ask, please.'

'O.K.' The dragon repeated the question, but his mind was not on it. He was watching a graceful sailing-boat coming down the harbour on her engine, her sails down and being furled by a young man. He rolled over on his front to see her the right way up. 'Give him a herring-aid,' said Adam.

'That's an expensive little job,' muttered the dragon.

'What d'you mean – a hearing-aid? You don't have to buy one, Dragon. It's only a riddle.'

'Adam,' observed the dragon. 'You are being stupid. I was referring to that yacht over there that's just coming towards us.'

Adam watched it for a moment, and then said he'd be off, and no sooner had he disappeared than the dragon heard a voice from the yacht, which was now quite near him.

'Hey, there!' came the voice.

'Hey yourself!' retorted the dragon.

'You there! You great green monster, whatever you are!'

'Are you referring to me, by any chance?' asked the dragon.

'I am. I've got stuff to unload and you're taking up half the quayside.'

'I am not.'

'You are, y'know.'

'The Harbour-Master gave me this mooring. *Personally.*'

'Don't believe you!'

The boat was very near now. The young man who had spoken was smartly dressed in white trousers, and a bright blue shirt. He leant over the side and said rather disagreeably: 'If you're going to be difficult, we'll fetch the Harbour-Master.'

'Do,' said the dragon carelessly, and added, as the young man turned away angrily: 'Did you know you'd been sitting in something nasty. Forgive me mentioning it.'

The fellow whipped round and looked down at his trousers' seat. 'Oh, damn!' he exclaimed. 'These were clean this morning. What the hell –'

'No need for bad language,' interrupted the dragon, in reproving tones. 'Weymouth likes to keep its harbour clean.'

'Oh, all right! We won't argue.'

'I'm not arguing,' said the dragon, with maddening calm.

'Jeff!' called the young man with the stain on his trousers' seat. He was speaking to a fair-haired chap standing in the cockpit with his hand on the tiller. 'Bring her round again, Jeff. We'll have to tie up alongside.'

After a few minutes, Jeff brought the yacht alongside the dragon and turned off the engine. His companion then threw a mooring rope onto the quay. Jeff, at the stern of the yacht, tossed another mooring rope, or warp, from his end. A couple of old sailors who were leaning on a rail, talking quietly, went over and fastened the warps to bollards, and there was the yacht securely tied up fore and aft.

The dragon watched all this with much interest – the first mooring rope had narrowly missed his ears. He was also able to take a good look at the two young men. The one standing in the bows. in his bright blue shirt and the crisp white trousers he was so proud of, obviously had quite different ideas about clothes from his companion's. Jeff's once-white shorts were dirty and patched, and his red T-shirt had a sizeable tear in the back of it. All the same, the dragon liked the look of the untidy Jeff better than his neat and rather bad-tempered friend.

'I wonder what the smart one's name is,' mused the dragon. 'Something rather classy like Sebastian, I expect,' and with this reflection he fell into a peaceful sleep, rocked gently on the incoming tide.

2

Baked Beans for Breakfast

R. DRAGON had concealed his first name for so many hundreds of years that he had no idea how irritating this was for people who wanted to greet him. They could only call out 'Ho, Dragon!' or 'Hullo there!' or they might cough and say awkwardly: 'I wonder if – er – Mr – er – that is – er – Dragon!'

When Adam brought his brother along the quay early next morning, the dragon, still half-asleep, heard them whispering: 'We'd better not wake him. Let's just leave it on the quay.'

Then the brother's voice came, much nearer: 'It certainly looks asleep.'

'It's *he* not *it*,' came Adam's higher-pitched, rather squeaky voice.

'Well, let's put it down here.'

'No, he won't see it there. Give it to me, John.'

What were they arguing about? Cautiously opening one eye, the dragon caught sight of a freckled arm and a hand clasping a brownish bottle.

'I want my breakfast and we've got to get that swim in first,' came John's voice. 'If it's asleep –'

'If *he's* asleep,' interrupted Adam.

'Oh, all right. If *he's* asleep . . . Oh, for heaven's sake put that bottle down, and let's get on.'

'Somebody might steal it,' said the dragon in a deep, growly voice.

Both boys jumped.

'Ho! Ho! That startled you, didn't it? Is that a bottle of sauce I see before me?' The dragon reached out a scaly paw and took the bottle from Adam, going on: 'How do you do? You're Adam's brother, I take it.'

'That's right. We've brought you some Daddy's Sauce.'

'Thank you. How very kind. Anything to go with it?'

'Well, no. 'Fraid not.'

'Never mind. It'll come in handy when I *do* have something to go with it, won't it? I suppose you've had –'

The dragon's words were interrupted by a noise behind him, coming from the yacht alongside. The cabin porthole opened jerkily and the voice said:

'D'you have to make such a row?'

'Sorry,' said the dragon. 'Are you both still asleep?'

'We were.'

'It's a lovely morning. I recommend you to get up like the boys here and have a swim.' The dragon beamed approvingly at John and Adam.

The porthole slammed shut.

'We'd better be going,' said John. 'We've got to have

this swim before breakfast. Mum seems to think it's fun for us.'

'So it is,' said the dragon, cheerfully. 'I invariably have a swim before breakfast when I'm in Cornwall.'

'It's not as cold here as it is along the esplanade,' said Adam, in a very disgruntled voice. 'And before breakfast, too. Don't you ever feel cold, Dragon?'

'Not often. I'm more or less centrally-heated.'

'Lucky you!' groaned John. 'Come on, Adam, let's get it over.'

'Grrr-r-h!' growled Adam between his teeth. 'I don't want a beastly swim before breakfast. Just because Mum used to do it when she was our age.'

John dragged his brother along the quay towards the esplanade.

'Enjoy yourselves!' cried the dragon and turned quickly to the yacht beside him. 'Sorry if I've woken you up again,' he called loudly, pressing his nose against the porthole.

'Go away!' came a muffled shout from within.

The dragon moved his head along to another porthole. This one had no curtains across it and looked into the galley, with its cooking-stove, sink, pots and pans and china. Standing on the cooker was an empty saucepan, with two tins of baked beans beside it.

'Must have been put there for breakfast,' thought the dragon, hungrily. He blew a tiny puff of green smoke against the metal rim of the porthole. Nothing happened. He held his breath for a few seconds and then let out another fiercer jet of smoke with a tiny red flame at its centre. This melted the metal frame of the porthole and the glass fell out into the harbour with a plop. The dragon then reached into the galley with his paw and extracted one of the tins of baked beans.

'How delicious! There's nothing nicer than baked beans,' he exclaimed to himself, and whipped the top off the can in a trice. The beans went down in one swallow and he poured the contents of the bottle of Daddy's Sauce after them, filled the bottle with water and sank it and the tin beneath him in the water. Tidiness was a virtue he learned at the court of King Arthur, where littei-louts were invariably beheaded.

He then turned and examined the boat that was moored beside him. It was about twenty-five foot long, not as long as the dragon if you counted in his tail. The hull was white, the sails bright red. The mainsail was rather carelessly bunched up along the boom, and the foresail was lying in a heap just behind the small bowsprit. By craning his neck round, the dragon could see the yacht's name painted on her stern: *Money-Spider*.

The time came when the two young men on board her wanted breakfast. One of them, the fair-haired one, got up, drew the curtain and opened the porthole of the cabin.

'It's a nice day, Maurice,' he called to his companion.

'Good-oh! Put the kettle on, will you?'

The dragon cocked his ear towards the boat. The men called out to each other as they dressed. One was still in the cabin where they slept, but the other was in the galley, getting the breakfast and pulling on his clothes at the same time.

'Are we getting any racing today?' asked the fair one, in the galley.

'Can't remember. We'll go up to the Club sometime

and find out. But we simply must – er – unload her first, Jeff. I don't want to start racing till that's done. Damn! I've cut my chin.'

The dragon stifled a chortling laugh, which was cut short by Jeff shouting: 'Maurice, I say! I thought there were two tins of baked beans.'

'There certainly were. I put 'em out last night.'

'There's only one here. Where did you put the second one?'

'On the stove, of course. It's probably fallen off.'

'No, it hasn't.'

'Well, I suppose I must have made a mistake and only put one out. The other'll be in the locker.'

'It isn't. What'll I do?'

'Stop making a fuss, Jeff. Open the tin. One'll do to start with. There's plenty of bread, isn't there?'

'We forgot to buy any.'

'*We* forgot? *You* forgot, you mean. Oh, for heaven's sake, go and buy some, Jeff.'

'You go, Maurice. You're more dressed than I am.'

'My chin's still bleeding, but O.K. And I'll get something to help out the beans – sausages or bacon or something.'

'Count me in,' murmured the dragon. 'Those baked beans weren't much of a breakfast.'

Maurice came on deck. He was a pleasant-looking chap, but almost too tidy and well-dressed, the dragon decided. He had a small beard and side-burns. His dark hair was rather long and curly. Today he was wearing bright blue trousers, and had on a white T-shirt with IT'S ME MAURICE printed on the chest. Without saying a word, Maurice stepped onto the dragon's back and

walked across him to the quay, onto which he bounded, using the dragon's neck as a springboard. When boats are moored side by side, as they often are in a busy harbour, the crews of the boats furthest from the quay step across the decks of the boats in between and nobody thinks anything of it, but it was a new idea to the dragon and he was both astonished and annoyed.

'Don't mind me,' he said loudly, as Maurice landed on the quay.

'What?' asked the young man, impatiently.

'I said: don't mind me.'

'Well, I didn't.'

'You don't ask whether you can tread on my back, do you?'

'If you don't like it, don't moor there.'

The dragon didn't know what to say to this, and before he could think of a really crushing reply, Maurice called out cheerfully: 'That's O.K. then, hey?' and he went off in the direction of the shops.

There are always sailors and fishermen by any harbourside who never appear to do anything but lean on rails and posts and bollards, and talk and watch and watch and talk. There were two such 'leaners' quite near the dragon. They had watched Maurice walk over his back and one of them now took his pipe out of his mouth, and pointing its stem at the dragon, observed: 'You be a bit large for our harbour, Mr Dragon.'

He was an old man, his brown face wrinkled with innumerable tiny lines. His mouth had only three teeth in front, each one rather like the post he was leaning against, brown and irregular, almost knotty. He wore faded and patched blue trousers, a fisherman's jersey and thick red knitted cap.

The dragon replied politely: 'Even a dragon has to have a mooring when he's in harbour.'

'Aye, but there's dragons and dragons, and harbours and harbours,' said the old man.

The dragon pondered this profound remark, and try as he would, he couldn't see what it meant, except exactly what it said, namely, that there are dragons and other dragons, and harbours and different harbours. There was a long pause during which the two Leaners smoked and watched the traffic of boats go by, with an occasional wave of the hand and a shout of greeting.

They appeared to have forgotten the dragon, who coughed to attract their notice and said: 'Certainly there are dragons and dragons. I am one –'

'Pleased to meet you,' said the Leaner with only three teeth.

'Then there's my aunt at Longleat, Aunt Dracula, and my cousin Fingal, who lives on the Scottish coast. I haven't seen him for two or three hundred years. As he only speaks Gaelic, I can't understand anything he says. So that makes three of us.'

The same man who had spoken before gazed open-mouthed at the dragon. 'An aunt at Longleat?' he repeated. 'And a cousin in Scotland, did I hear you say?'

'It makes three,' said the dragon. 'Like your teeth.'

The old man looked amazed at the dragon's knowledge of arithmetic.

'Three dragons. Three teeth,' observed the dragon.

'That's got you, George,' cried the other old man, hitherto silent. 'That's got you. Oh, I like that, I do. I always did say as how you ought to get yourself a pair of false gnashers like me.' He pointed to his own mouth where gleamed two rows of teeth, large and square and rather like small tombstones.

'How interesting!' cried the dragon. 'I've got false-er-gnashers as well. I haven't put them in yet,' he went on. 'I keep them in a long box.'

'In a box? What d'ye do that for, then, Dragon?'

'I – well, to be truthful, I wasn't very popular in days long ago. I – er – used to eat the odd maiden. Or two. Or three.'

'Cor!' exclaimed the three-toothed one. 'That's O.K.

by me, mate. I can think of two or three women as would be better eaten.'

'Tut! Tut!' cried the dragon, disapprovingly. 'I wouldn't dream of eating anyone now. I'm a reformed dragon.'

'You ain't met 'em yet,' said the other old sailor. 'There's George's wife, Daisy, for instance.'

'Nonsense!' said the dragon, briskly. 'I am certainly not going to eat George's wife Daisy. I never heard of such a thing. You'll be asking me to eat *your* wife next.'

'I ain't got a wife,' said the old man. 'I ain't married, thank the Lord.'

The dragon decided not to go on with this conversation.

'Why don't we introduce ourselves?' he suggested. 'I'm R. Dragon.'

'I'm Bill Pouncy,' said the one with the 'gnashers', 'and this here chap with three teeth – oh, that were good – the quick way you counted! - he's George Snook.'

'Very pleased to meet you both,' said the dragon, graciously.

At this moment Maurice appeared, carrying three large bags in his arms.

'Mind if I cross over your back again?' he asked.

'Not at all,' answered the dragon, and added, much pleased by Maurice's change of heart: 'Could I ask you where you obtained those bags of – er –'

'Ready-cooked hot sausages in this one,' replied Maurice. 'Loaf of bread in here and a couple of meat pies in that one. Got 'em at the bakery round the corner.'

'Really?' said the dragon, his mouth watering. 'I must try it.'

'They've lots more. Here, have a sausage.' Maurice handed one to the dragon. 'Have two, in fact. Or three.'

The dragon was very pleased and thanked him politely as he bit into the first sausage and munched it up in his toothless jaws. Maurice crossed over his back and went down into the galley.

'Pardon me,' said the dragon, putting his eye to the open porthole. 'Might I borrow the mustard?'

The other young man, Jeff, who was laying a small table for breakfast, handed the mustard to the dragon, saying: 'Here it is – feel free.'

The dragon scooped up a clawful.

'Come on, Maurice, I'm hungry. Empty out the bags. The coffee's just about ready.'

The dragon heard no more of their conversation, as he had turned back to talk to his new friends, the two Leaners, Bill and George. Most of the people the dragon met, like the Harbour-Master and the Leaners and the yachtsmen, were not really surprised to find a dragon in their midst. Seafaring men get used to anything – dragons, whales, mermaids, giant sharks, they're none of them unusual or unbelievable to a sailor. And there was something special in the air of Weymouth. It got under people's coats and hats and jerseys and whirled their wits round like spinning-tops. This made the world seem such an exciting place that nothing could surprise them.

That was why the Secretary of the Yacht Club wasn't in the least astonished when *he* saw the dragon. He came past on his way to the Club House and didn't even wait to be introduced.

'Good morning! Good morning!' he cried. 'Delighted to see a dragon in the harbour at last. And a green one, too. Splendid! Have you had the Harbour-Master's permission to moor here, my good dragon?'

'Certainly I have, and what's more –'

The Secretary didn't give him time to finish his words. He went on, almost in the same breath: 'Always delighted to see you at the Club, Dragon.' Then, turning to the Leaners, he said: 'I see *Money-Spider*'s in port again.'

He waved his hand towards the yacht next to the dragon, who at once called out, helpfully: 'Yes, that's right. The crew are a couple of –'

'Jeff and Maurice,' interrupted the Secretary. 'I know 'em well. Nice chaps. Very nice young chaps.'

'Maurice seems to think he's got a right of way across my –' began the dragon, getting annoyed, but the Secretary never gave anyone a chance to finish a sentence.

'Don't give it a thought, my dear dragon,' he said. Then he suddenly stood quite still and sniffed. 'Lovely smell of fish from that bar over there,' he observed. 'Reminds me of my breakfast. My, it was an excellent one this morning.'

'What was it?' asked the dragon quickly, but the Secretary was already walking away, very fast. 'What was it?' the dragon called out again, and the Secretary stopped in his tracks, swivelled round and made a megaphone of his hands. 'Mackerel!' he shouted. 'Fresh mackerel! Get one of the fishermen to let you have a couple straight off his boat. Nothing like 'em!'

'How much?' bellowed the dragon.

'Two lovely fresh mackerel at ten pence each. Food for the gods!'

'I'd need four, if not six,' thought the dragon, and he was just lifting up his nose and smelling the delectable smells from the fishbar that were wafted across the harbour from the opposite quay, when John and Adam appeared. They were half running, half stumbling along the quay. Their hair was wet and clung to their heads. Adam had his swimming trunks wrapped up in a very grubby, sandy towel. John carried his in a beach bag.

'We can't stop, Dragon,' called out John as they passed. 'Got to get back to breakfast.'

'Had a nice swim?' inquired the dragon.

'Not bad. Terribly cold when you first go in.'

'Just as bad when you come out,' spluttered Adam, out of breath and his teeth chattering. But as John hurried on, Adam ran up to the dragon and panted: 'D'you know – puff – what the sea said – pant – when it – puff-puff – reached the seashore?'

'I do not,' replied the dragon.

'Nothing!' cried Adam, with a shriek of laughter. 'Nothing! It just WAVED!' He waved to the dragon himself and ran down the quay after his brother, shouting: 'Gosh! Do I want breakfast?'

3
Laws and Luggage

'Hi!'

The dragon's ears twitched. He was dozing by the quay.

'Hi, there!' came the voice again.

The dragon woke up from a dream of sugared buns and baked beans to see the Harbour-Master's launch drawn up beside him.

'Might it not be more nautical to cry "Ahoy, there!" or – er – "Belay!"?' asked the dragon and he spoke rather peevishly, for it had been a beautiful dream and now it was gone forever.

'It doesn't matter what I call out,' retorted the Harbour-Master. 'You can't occupy this berth for longer than twenty-four hours. Time's up. I've allowed you to moor at this quay for free, just for one night. Now you must go or else pay the harbour dues.'

'No problem,' replied the dragon, calmly. 'I can afford to pay you. If it's a fair price, of course.' He withdrew from inside one huge green ear a leather wallet which he flipped open with a claw. 'What's the damage for one week?' he asked airily, displaying a small wad of one-pound notes.

'Hullo-ullo!' exclaimed the Harbour-Master. 'Where did you get all that money?'

'Here and there,' replied the dragon. 'Up and down and round about. People are extremely careless with money. I think that they probably have far too much. Certainly their children do. Now when I was a dragon cub, I only got –'

'Never mind when you were a cub. You mean you picked this money up?'

'That's right. You've got the idea. The summer season in Cornwall is a rich field. Parents give their children 10p, 20p, even 50p, for ice-creams and lollies and whatever, and the silly cubs – I mean kids – drop half the coins as they scramble over the sands and rocks. Then they set up a howl so that I know pretty well where they've dropped them. Later on, I find the coins. It's as simple as that.'

'Really?' commented the Harbour-Master. 'You go round scrabbling in the sand for coins, do you?'

'I do *not* scrabble,' replied the dragon haughtily. 'I have a metal-detector. I just pass it over the sands in likely places, when I stroll over the sands of an evening. It's amazing what I pick up – corkscrews, nails, tinfoil (very useful), watches, even rings and, of course, coins. I've half-furnished my cave with some of the objects I've picked up on the beach.'

'All right. If you pay the harbour dues, you can stay for a week,' said the Harbour-Master, still staring at the one-pound notes.

'How much?' asked the dragon.

'I'd just like to point out that you are very large and very long. You occupy about two berths. By rights you should pay double.'

'By whose rights?' demanded the dragon, quickly. 'By *my* rights you ought to feel so honoured to have a dragon in your small and insignificant harbour –'

'Never mind that,' interrupted the Harbour-Master. 'You just –'

But the dragon was determined to have his say, and went on: 'You ought, by my rights, to be paying me to stay here. I'm a tourist attraction.' He gave a beaming smile and green smoke trickled out of his jaws and floated over the Harbour-Master's head.

'O.K.,' said this officer, with a slight smile. 'I'll admit that Weymouth's in the news this morning because of your arrival, so I'll make it a special cheap fee – 50p for the week. How's that?'

'Wicked,' groaned the dragon. 'Daylight robbery, but here you are.' With a delicate claw, he selected a one-pound note from his wallet and handed it to the Harbour-Master. Then he went on: 'I haven't got the right change. I've a good friend, a lobster-fisherman, who changes the coins I pick up into one-pound notes. A heavy bag of coins in one ear would be most uncomfortable.'

'Well, you'll have to have a 50p piece now – the change from your pound note. Here you are.'

The dragon tucked the coin into the purse part of his wallet, which he then replaced in his left ear. The Harbour-Master revved up his engine and started to move away, first saying: 'My Assistant, Mr Tanner, will be along this morning to register you. By rights –'

'You're always talking about rights. Whose rights this time?'

'Weymouth harbour rights. You ought to register at my office, but you couldn't get through the door, so I'll send Mr Tanner along with the papers.' And with that, the Harbour-Master disappeared in the direction of the harbour mouth, where a red-funnelled Channel boat was just leaving the pier.

The young men on *Money-Spider* were talking, and the dragon now heard Jeff ask: 'Well, what shall we do this morning?'

'Pull yourself together, Jeff,' retorted his companion. 'You know the routine. The sooner we get unloaded, the happier I'll be.'

'Yes, of course. I hadn't really forgotten. Let's go along the quay and see if he's there.'

'What's the time?'

'Getting on for eleven.'

'O.K., let's go. He must have opened the shop by now.'

The two young men came up on deck, and asked politely if they might step across the dragon's back.

'Charmed!' cried the dragon, who was feeling in a very good humour, for he had thought that the harbour dues would have been much more expensive. 'Mind my spikes!' he added. 'I'd better get a doormat so that you can wipe your feet first. Ho! Ho!'

Maurice and Jeff laughed as well, and Maurice said: 'Get a doormat with WELCOME on it –'

'Or BLESS THIS HOUSE,' interrupted Jeff.

'Or R. DRAGON – HIS MAT,' bellowed the dragon, full of the joys of life and pleased that the two young men were going to be his friends.

'We'll see if we can buy you one in the town,' cried Jeff as they went off down the quay.

When they had gone, the dragon noticed that there was a cat sitting on the quay, staring at him. It was a plump, sleek cat, with very pretty tabby markings, like a mackerel – which reminded the dragon that he must ask Jeff and Maurice to cook him some mackerel for breakfast. Perhaps, he thought, I'd better offer to pay for two extra for them to eat. Or four extra. I don't want to appear mean.

The cat was staring at him as though it could read his thoughts. Now the dragon was not well acquainted with cats, because they do not often visit rocks and sandy sea-shores. He did remember that he had met several cats in the far-off days when he had lived at the court of King Arthur, and had an idea that you called all cats 'Puss', so he held out one paw rather uncertainly and called out: 'Pussy! Puss–puss!'

The cat immediately turned its back and started to lick its stomach.

'Puss! Pretty puss!' The dragon tried to draw the cat towards him with a beckoning claw. The creature stopped washing itself for a moment, turned its head and gave the dragon a scornful glance. It then went back to its morning wash, this time attacking a back leg, which it stuck into the air like a bollard.

At this moment the Harbour-Master's Assistant came along the quay and exclaimed: 'Hullo, Sybil-puss! How's life with you?'

The cat immediately began to weave in and out of his feet, rubbing against his trouser-legs. The dragon felt mortified.

'It seems to know you,' he said, gloomily.

'Of course she knows me. We all know Sybil. She's the cat from the café along there. Sybil owns *this* part of the quay, don't you, Sybil?'

'Oh, does she?' said the dragon, watching the wreath-ings and writhings of the mackerel-like cat.

'You must make friends with her,' said the Assistant. 'I expect she came along to inspect you.'

'Inspect me?'

'Yes, she's pretty fussy who she has on the quay,' said the young man, fondling Sybil's ears. The cat promptly rolled over and waved its legs in the air. The dragon looked on disapprovingly while the fellow rubbed Sybil's orange-coloured stomach.

'What an exhibition!' muttered the dragon. 'I can't see myself lying on *my* back and waving my legs in the air.'

'Well, we must get to business,' said the Assistant, letting Sybil go with obvious reluctance. 'I'm fond of cats,' he added, giving the animal one more affectionate stroke. Then he turned to the dragon.

'There are just one or two things we have to ask,' he said. 'I've brought a form –' He felt in his pockets.

'A beautiful morning, isn't it?' said the dragon.

'If you wouldn't mind, Sir,' began the Assistant, squatting down on the quayside near the dragon's head, and opening out some papers. He took a pen from his breast-pocket. 'First – the name in full.'

'I'm full all right,' said the dragon, smiling a broad smile as he remembered his breakfast. 'My name? Dragon. R. Dragon.'

'If I could just have what the R. stands for, Sir,' asked the Assistant.

'Ah, no. I can't tell you that.'

'It's necessary, I'm afraid, Sir.'

'Not to me it isn't.'

'It is for us.'

'Why?' argued the dragon. 'You're not likely to have any other dragons in your harbour, are you?'

'I don't suppose so, Sir,' said the unhappy Assistant, who had started drawing a dragon's head on the paper in his agitation. 'All the same, we have to have the full name. That's what it says here.'

'Rubbish!' snorted the dragon. 'I never give my full name to anyone, except my nearest and dearest. Like the mermaid who lives in Kynance Cove. She knows it and so does my old friend, Sue.'

Mr Tanner wrinkled his brows. 'Well, I don't rightly know what to put,' he said.

'Quite simple. Just put R. Dragon.'

Mr Tanner wrote it down on the form. 'Home address?' he went on.

'The Cave, Constantine Bay, Cornwall,' answered the dragon.

'It hasn't got a number, I suppose?' asked the young man, hopefully.

'Caves don't have numbers, my good fellow. Just Cornwall would find me, if it comes to that.'

Mr Tanner wrote it down carefully. 'Purpose of visit?' he asked.

'Now, what shall we say?' mused the dragon. 'Curiosity, I think.'

'Shall we say pleasure?' suggested the Assistant.

'Well, I don't know if it's pleasure or not, do I?' said the dragon, adding, with a sniff of disapproval: 'It certainly won't be pleasure if you ask me many more questions.'

'I'm sorry, Sir, but it's the harbour bye-laws.'

'Oh, bother the bye-laws!' exclaimed the dragon.

'Tonnage? That comes next,' said Mr Tanner, a quaver in his voice.

The dragon gave a bellow of laughter and rolled about so much that great waves crossed the harbour and all the moored yachts tossed up and down. Someone tied up to the quay opposite rushed up on deck and shouted:

'Who the hell's making all these waves? My coffee's spilt all over my trousers and the kettle's fallen off the stove. It's outrageous! I shall complain to the Harbour-Master.'

'Ho! Ho!' boomed the dragon.

The man on the other side couldn't see the dragon properly because *Money-Spider* was in the way, but he heard the dragon's loud laugh, and he could see Mr Tanner standing on the quay.

'You there! You, young man!' he shouted. 'I'm Colonel Ocklestone. I'll report you to the Harbour-Master for not doing your duty properly. You've allowed some careless fool to come through the harbour at about twenty knots. Nearly capsized me!' With that he disappeared into his cabin.

The Harbour-Master's Assistant bent down to the dragon's ear.

'Actually,' he said, 'you want to beware of Colonel Ocklestone and his wife. They've been here for the last three years and they're a headache, I can tell you, and not very handy with a boat either. They've caused a lot of trouble.'

'They'd better not cause trouble with me,' snorted the dragon. 'Now what were we talking about? Tonnage, wasn't it? Well, you'd better weigh me, hadn't you? Ho! Ho!'

Mr Tanner looked nonplussed. 'I'll put down two tons,' he said. Glancing down at his papers, he added, with relief: 'I don't think the rest of this applies to you. Oh, half a minute! Yes, there's one very important question. The Harbour-Master said I must be sure and ask you this. Are you a British dragon?'

'What d'you think I am?' demanded the dragon, indignantly.

'Well, you could have come from abroad, of course, even if you were British. I ought to have asked you where you were last in port – France, for instance, or – or Holland?'

'I think you must be mad, asking these silly questions,' said the dragon. 'Or is this some idiotic game? I have come from my cave in Cornwall. First, I flew over from the north coast to the south, and I came down in the sea just outside Plymouth. Then I sailed into the harbour, past Plymouth Ho! Ho!'

'Excuse me, Sir, but isn't it just Plymouth Hoe?'

'No, it isn't. Drake played a game of bowls there, I once read, and when someone told him the Spanish Armada was sailing up the Channel, he just said: "Let 'em come, Ho! Ho!" and went on playing bowls. Exactly what *I* should have done in the circumstances. And that's why it's called Plymouth Ho! Ho! to this day.'

The young man thought he'd better not argue. He wrote down Plymouth and left it at that.

'Why d'you want to know if I'm British, anyway?' asked the dragon.

'It's the rabies laws, Sir.'

'Never heard of 'em.'

'No animals allowed into a British port from a foreign country, Sir.'

'What d'you do with them? Make them wait in the Channel?'

'No, Sir. We put them into quarantine.'

'As if they had mumps? You're not putting *me* into quarantine,' said the dragon. 'Not if I had measles and scarlet fever and chicken-pox all rolled into one.' He folded his front paws over his chest and blew a puff of green smoke from his nostrils.

'Oh, no, Sir, of course not. There's no need.'

'You wouldn't put me into quarantine even if there was a need,' said the dragon, firmly.

'Well, it's fortunate we haven't got to, isn't it? Thank you very much, Sir. You've been most helpful. The only thing I've got to ask you is – er – not to throw your rubbish into the harbour, and to see that you are securely moored whenever you're at the quay.'

'All that's quite unnecessary and rather insulting,' said the dragon, frowning severely. 'It's obvious that you have had no experience of dragons.'

'Well, no, Sir. I haven't.'

'Now's your chance,' observed the dragon, and unfolded his paws.

The Harbour-Master's Assistant put his hand to his peaked cap in a salute and began to walk back towards the pier and the Channel boats. Sybil, who had been listening to the conversation, got up, stretched and walked along with him, her tail in the air like a ship's mast.

'Just a minute!' called the dragon.

Mr Tanner and Sybil both turned round.

'How far away is the railway station?'

42

'The station?' faltered Mr Tanner. 'You're not think-ing of going anywhere by train, are you?' The thought of the dragon trying to get into a railway carriage was almost too much for him.

'Of course not. Why should I? I've only just arrived.'

'The station's down that way, beyond the Town Bridge.' Mr Tanner pointed. 'If you just follow the rail-way lines, you'll get there.'

'Thank you very much!' called the dragon. 'I want to pick up my luggage. I sent it by rail from Plymouth Ho! Ho!'

'I must get back to the office,' said Mr Tanner hastily. He didn't want to find himself going round to the station to collect the dragon's luggage, whatever that might be.

The dragon heaved himself out of the water onto the quay. Luckily the tide was in and the water high, only a foot or so below the edge of the quay. He couldn't have climbed out like this at low tide, as he was to discover later. He shook himself, beginning with his head and ears. Then the shake rippled down his backbone right to the tip of his green tail. Quantities of harbour water sprayed off him, some of it onto parked cars. The dragon looked rather guilty about this but after all, he told himself, the sun was hot. The cars would soon dry and be all the better for a free carwash.

He walked down to the bridge and underneath it. Beyond was the Backwater. It looked like a huge lake, but in reality it was part of the mouth of the River Wey. It was packed with craft, most of them small dinghies and speedboats and motor launches, craft for which there wasn't room in the harbour itself, which was reserved for the fishing fleet and large yachts which couldn't sail under the bridge.

The railway line ran along the edge of the quay past a big car park, some public gardens and an amusement centre. The dragon was interested in all that he saw. It was so different from Constantine Bay, with its sand-dunes and rocks. Although sailors and fishermen saw nothing amazing about a dragon walking along the quay, some of the visitors whom he met were astonished, while others were frightened and ran away with gasps and shrieks, of which the dragon took no notice. A few simply refused to believe their eyes and muttered about sunstroke or too much beer.

'It's a dragon! No, it can't be! Oh, Lord, why did I eat that lobster last night?' groaned one elderly man, clasping his stomach. 'I ought to have known I would pay for it.'

'Serve you right!' said his wife, disagreeably, but she took her husband's arm, and hurried him past the dragon. 'You never know,' she muttered. 'Perhaps I'm seeing things, too.'

'Now, come along, Dora!' cried a fat woman in a tight, flowered dress, pulling the little girl whose hand she held towards the dragon. 'You needn't be afraid if I'm with you, and think how nice it will be to tell your mummy and daddy that you've seen a sea-serpent.'

'It'll bite me! I know it will bite me!' screamed the child.

'No, it won't. Come along, Dora, you're nearly pulling my arm off.'

'I won't come! It's a horrible monster!' whined Dora.

'It won't hurt you. Auntie'll speak to it. You'll see.'

She was a comfortable, stupid sort of woman who

hadn't the wit to suspect that a dragon might be dangerous. If Weymouth Council let a dragon roam about among the trippers, then it must be all right. (She finally met her end by being eaten by a lion that had escaped from a travelling circus. She thought *that* belonged to Weymouth Council, too.)

The dragon thought she was not only silly but extremely ugly. He smiled at frightened little Dora, who was a pretty child, and said: 'No need to be afraid of me, Dora. I don't eat people any more. Eating people is wrong. Look, I'll show you something. Just watch.' And the dragon put his head back and blew a whole set of green smoke rings, one after the other.

Dora was enchanted and clapped her hands. 'Lovely! Lovely!' she cried. 'What a nice dragon you are! Don't be frightened, Auntie, I'll take care of you.'

'I'll whisper a secret idea I've had, if you'll put your ear close to my mouth,' said the dragon.

'You'll do nothing of the sort!' exclaimed the aunt, who felt that her authority over Dora was slipping. 'I've told you often enough not to speak to strangers.'

'He blew green smoke rings for me!' shrieked Dora, and before Auntie could stop her, she ran up to the dragon and put her ear close to his mouth. The dragon whispered quickly: 'I don't like your aunt.'

'Neither do I,' whispered Dora.

'Shall we push her into the Backwater?' suggested the dragon, who was sometimes rather heartless.

Dora had been brought up properly and knew that it was not a good idea to push people. least of all your relations, into any sort of water. 'That's being naughty,' she whispered. Then the fat woman grabbed her and pulled her away. The dragon sighed. 'A pity,' he called out to Dora. 'She'd have made a lovely big splash!' And Dora looked back at him and giggled. He blew another ring for her, and then went into the railway station. He caused rather a commotion among the passengers who were waiting for a train. The ticket-collector said: 'Where's your ticket, then? You can't go onto the platform without a ticket.'

'I've called for some luggage,' explained the dragon.

'Oh, luggage, is it? You want to go along to that door labelled PARCELS.'

The dragon padded along as directed and the man inside the Parcels Office peered at him through rather grimy spectacles that had slipped halfway down his nose, and asked him what he wanted.

'My luggage,' said the dragon. 'I sent it here from Plymouth Ho! Ho!'

'Hoe,' corrected the man.

'Ho! Ho!' repeated the dragon.

'I'm not here to have a laughing match with you, you know,' said Parcels Office, firmly. 'I got my work to do. If you want to have a good laugh, go along to the buffet and ask for a sandwich. That'll make you laugh.'

'Thank you,' said the dragon. politely. 'When I want a laugh, that's where I'll go. Meanwhile, I want my luggage.'

'What's the name?'

'R. Dragon. I paid in advance for it to come here.'

'What is it, then? Suitcase? Wooden crate? Or what?'

'It's three things,' said the dragon. 'There's a small suitcase. That's got my teeth in it, my handkerchiefs and one or two oddments – a woolly hat for wearing when

46

it's windy, for instance. Tied to the suitcase is a green rug. There is also a cage.'

'What sort of cage?'

'A parrot-cage.'

'With a parrot in it?'

'Not yet. I'm hoping to buy a parrot from a sailor.'

'Oh. Half a mo' and I'll look. Shouldn't be difficult to find.' The man disappeared and came back with the suitcase and the parrot-cage. 'Here you are,' he said triumphantly. 'You can trust British Rail. All shipshape and Bristol-fashion, as my old father used to say.'

'Plymouth-fashion would be better,' said the dragon, giving him a genial smile.

'Now we won't have any more of that Plymouth Ho! Ho! stuff,' said the Parcels man, sternly. 'Here you are.

One suitcase with green rug attached and one parrot-cage. Please sign here.'

He handed a pen to the dragon, who signed his name in the Parcels book, and picked up his luggage.

'Hooray! Now I can make myself really comfortable,' he thought, and as he strolled back along the quay, he sang a sea-shanty, to the admiration of all who heard him.

> 'Oh, say were you ever on Weymouth quay?
>   Oh . . . Weymouth!
> It's there that the river runs down to the sea,
> And I'm bound for Weymouth quay.
>   So it's heave up my bag,
>   Way down Weymouth!
>   Up with my luggage
>   And up with my cage,
> And I'm bound for Weymouth quay!'

As he reached the Town Bridge, he thought of another verse, and started singing again. His voice boomed and echoed against the stone arches of the bridge, as he walked under it. People leaned over parapets, and came out of cafés, and stopped their cars, to see who was singing. This pleased the dragon very much.

> 'Now, who's got a parrot to sell me today?
>   Oh . . . Weymouth!
> An African parrot with feathers of grey . . .'

But here the dragon was stuck. 'It's got a red tail,' he muttered to himself, 'but I don't think I can make that fit in. Bother!'

However, he could now see his mooring berth ahead of him, and the Leaners were waving to him. Bill Pouncy called out: 'That's a fine parrot-cage you got there!'

'It needs a parrot in it,' said the dragon. 'I'd like a grey African parrot. With a red tail. It'd keep me company in my lonely cave in Cornwall.'

'Ah!' said Mr Snook, and went on chewing something with his toothless gums. Both men came over and examined the parrot-cage thoughtfully.

'Didn't Sailor Pearce have one of they red-tailed parrots?'

'Aye, he did, a' believe.'

'Where's he now, Sailor Pearce?'

'Over in Portland, got some job there.'

'Next time we see him, we'll mention it,' said the toothless Leaner, George Snook. 'I did hear him say he were thinking of getting rid of his parrot. His wife didn't like it.'

'Maybe the parrot didn't like Sailor's wife?' suggested Bill Pouncy.

'Ah, could be,' agreed George, and both old men fell silent. They said no more about getting a parrot, but no doubt they were thinking about it, as they stood and smoked and watched the traffic of the harbour.

The dragon opened his suitcase and peered in.

'Ah, good!' he exclaimed. 'My woolly hat. I might wear it at night. It's a bit chilly then. And there are my teeth. I'll put them at the top. Never know when I might need 'em.'

He closed down the top of his suitcase and put it with the bird-cage on the edge of the quay, close beside him when he'd secured his mooring rope and was back in the water again.

4

The *Money-Spider* Mystery

THE dragon had enjoyed exploring the Backwater and finding the railway station, but it had been a tiring day. He was not used to tramping round a town. He lived very quietly in his cave in Constantine Bay in Cornwall, just taking a stroll over the sands and rocks on most evenings. As for longer journeys like a visit to his friend, the mermaid of Kynance Cove, of course he used his wings, for flying is less exhausting for a dragon than walking. And so is swimming. But you can't fly or swim through a town.

He had brought his luggage back successfully, and an awkward job it had been with a suitcase *and* a parrot-cage. Now he needed his afternoon rest. The dragon was a great believer in afternoon naps. He lumbered slowly along the quay. He couldn't get into the water at his mooring, because the tide was rather low so he decided to jump in, and jump in he did – with a colossal splash. The waves rose so high for a few minutes that it looked as if the harbour had been struck by a tidal wave. Small boats tossed up and down and even large ones rocked on their moorings. The dragon cheered up and felt quite bright at seeing the commotion he had caused. He shook the water out of his ears and began to swim to his berth, nearby.

Suddenly he heard Colonel Ocklestone shouting angrily from his yacht which was moored almost directly opposite, and was still bouncing up and down.

'What on earth d'you think you're doing? You – you there – whoever you are on that yacht with a fancy figure-head! Your boat's much too big to be moored in this part of the harbour. You're a danger to shipping! I shall report you! I'll have the law on you!'

The dragon realized that the Colonel took him to be some sort of ship. He looked thoughtfully at the indignant officer's yacht and saw that it was aptly named the *Furious*. He then made a mental note that he would get much pleasure from boring a hole in the *Furious* one dark night, a hole well below the water-line, and he was just drifting along, absorbed in this alluring though rather wicked idea, when the Colonel shouted: 'Why don't you show yourself, whoever you are who's in charge of that green boat? I've a good mind to go and see the Harbour-Master straight away. Yes, by Gad, that's what I'll do. No time like the present.'

He began to cross the deck of the boat nearest the quay, alongside which his yacht *Furious* was moored. It was more than the dragon could bear. Swivelling his long body round in the water, he ducked his head, dived and

came up dripping and puffing within a few feet of
Colonel Ocklestone, who at that moment had one foot
on the boatdeck and the other stretched out on the
rung of an iron ladder fastened to the side of the quay.
The Colonel's china-blue eyes bulged with astonishment
and his white moustache and side-whiskers blew out-
wards like a cake-frill round his red face when he saw
the dragon's head surfacing above the water close by him.
A few seconds later he gave a strangled cry, grabbed
wildly at the ladder, missed it and fell into the water
with a loud KERBLUNK! As he came up, gasping
and threshing his arms about, the dragon said coolly:
'Who's making a splash now?'

The unfortunate Colonel floundered and sank again. He was, alas, no swimmer. The dragon now slightly regretted the trick he'd played, so he held out a relenting paw, saying: 'Here you are, Colonel. Hang on and I'll pull you back to your own boat.'

The bemused man clutched the dragon's paw and found himself pulled across to his yacht by what seemed to him an extraordinary boat with no one visible on board, no mast or sails, and a talking figure-head shaped like a dragon's. Suddenly it dawned upon him that it must indeed be a dragon and not a boat at all. What is more, he clearly saw with his own eyes a gentle grin upon the creature's face. He scrambled onto the deck of his boat, looked round for a moment and saw a green back with yellow fins disappearing across the harbour. The Colonel's smart white trousers were ruined, his bright blue blazer with its brass buttons was soaked and stained brown with harbour water. He stood for a moment, panting and dripping, while his wife came up from the cabin, crying: 'Oh, my goodness gracious! Whatever's happened, Percy?'

'A dragon!' spluttered the Colonel. 'There's a – a – *dragon* in the harbour!'

'Rubbish, dear! There's no such thing. Come along down to the cabin. I knew you'd had too much to drink at lunch. I told you so, didn't I?'

Meanwhile, laughing to himself, the dragon had reached his mooring, and tied himself to his bollard with the piece of rope. *Money-Spider* luckily was not there as Maurice and Jeff had gone sailing in Weymouth Bay, after finding the shop they wanted was shut. Though Maurice had argued and objected when Jeff suggested it, saying that he didn't want to sail until they were 'unloaded', Jeff had in the end persuaded him to take the boat out. It was a perfect day with a steady but not too stiff a breeze, and Maurice had enjoyed it so much that he sailed much further down the coast than he had meant to, to Jeff's great joy. They didn't return until the evening. By then the dragon was asleep, lying on his back with his forepaws folded over his chest, and his long tail rising and falling with the movement of the water.

He woke up once, soon after midnight, to see the Boat-train coming very slowly along the quay close beside him. The station was right in Weymouth town, about half a mile along the Backwater, as the dragon had found out when he went to collect his luggage. Passengers travelling to the Channel Isles, however, stayed in their train seats and were carried past the main railway station and along the quay to the pier where the red-funnelled Channel boats berthed. The train had a man walking in front of it, to warn people to get off the rails. He was called the flagman, because he carried a red flag as a warning to stop the slow-moving train if he saw an obstacle on the line. Not only might people and dogs be on the railway track, but often cars were parked across it, in spite of notices telling drivers that this was not allowed. The dragon had seen the Channel Boat-train several times now. He much enjoyed watching it roll past him at a snail's pace – it was not permitted to travel at more than four miles an hour – and often waved to the passengers. Tonight the engine-driver recognized him and called out: 'Hullo, there, Dragon! Time you was asleep, m'dear.'

Next morning, the dragon woke up late to hear the voices of Maurice and Jeff as they dressed.

'I'll make a shopping list while I'm shaving. You know, I still wonder where that tin of baked beans went to, a few days ago.'

'I suppose you really did look everywhere?'

'I think so.'

'Well, don't let it worry you. It'll turn up.'

'It won't. I took it,' confessed the dragon in a hollow voice.

Maurice, who had just come into the galley, peered out at him through the porthole. '*You* took it? Well, I'll be –'

He was about to explode with annoyance but the dragon interrupted him with the words: 'Please forgive me.' He turned his large eyes upon the young man with an extremely contrite expression and went on: 'I was tired and hungry. I am not by nature a dragon who steals tins of baked beans or anything else. I'll gladly pay you for the tin. How much?'

'Well,' began Maurice, softened by this speech. 'I think those tins cost –'

'Oh, for heaven's sake, Maurice!' shouted Jeff. 'Surely we can spare him a tin of baked beans?'

'Thank you,' said the dragon. 'It's very nice of you but I prefer to pay my way.'

'No, we'll give you the beans. We insist,' said Maurice. 'Say no more about them. I wish we knew how that porthole cover disappeared, though. You didn't eat that, did you, Dragon?'

The dragon hesitated. 'Well, I haven't exactly eaten it,' he said. 'But – er – there was an accident. I yawned in its direction and my breath being very hot and dragonish melted the iron rim and the glass fell out. Plop!'

Though this was not strictly true, the dragon felt that it was true enough to pass muster. He heard Jeff say: 'Well, Mr Burrell will fit another one quite quickly, if he's not too busy.'

'I'm not keen to take the boat to Burrell's yard just yet,' came Maurice's voice. 'Not until she's unloaded.'

Unloaded? That word again. The dragon made a mental note that he *must* find out what it meant.

'Breakfast ready?' came Jeff's voice.

The dragon suddenly murmured to himself a motto that he'd often found useful in the past: Nothing venture, nothing have. Quickly he rolled over onto his front, ferreted in his left ear and brought out his wallet. Then, turning his head round so that one gleaming yellow eye looked directly into the porthole, straight at Maurice, he gave a little cough. Hrrrrm!

Maurice looked up and dropped the fork he was prodding the bacon with.

'My hat! You gave me a surprise,' he exclaimed.

'I'm sorry,' said the dragon. 'If you're staying here long, you'll have to get used to me, won't you?'

'Anything you want, or were you just looking in out of curiosity? Sorry I can't invite you onto the boat, ha! ha! but you're about twice her size.'

'I could give *you* a personally conducted tour round me, Ho! Ho! at tuppence a trip!' snorted the dragon.

Maurice laughed and called Jeff again.

'Can't come for a mo',' came Jeff's voice. 'I can't find the T-shirt I want –'

The dragon called out: 'D'you mean the one with BRAIN OF BRITAIN on it?'

'That's the one.'

'It's –' began the dragon and stopped. He had had a bright idea. 'This is a stroke of luck for me,' he muttered to himself, extracting his wallet again and taking a pound note from it.

'Would you let me buy Jeff's breakfast?' he asked Maurice. 'I'm starving, and you'll have time to cook him another while he's searching for his T-shirt. You see –' the dragon lowered his voice to a whisper – 'You see, Jeff's T-shirt with BRAIN OF BRITAIN on it isn't in the cabin at all. Actually it's hanging from the rigging.'

Maurice exploded with laughter. 'You are a card, Dragon,' he said. 'Of course, I remember –' he whispered this, joining in the conspiracy – 'Jeff washed it last night and hung it there to dry. You're a one for your food, aren't you, Dragon?'

'The staff of life,' murmured the dragon, 'and don't pretend *you* don't like your food. Just a minute, Maurice. Before you hand me that delicious looking plate of eggs and bacon, would you put a dob of mustard on it, as before?'

'Right! There you are. But I can't possibly take a pound off you, Dragon. It's far too much.'

'Could we come to a little arrangement?' asked the dragon, clutching his plate and longing to start. This was the idea he'd had when he'd repeated the motto: Nothing venture, nothing have. 'Will you keep my pound note and give me breakfast for as long as it lasts? May I suggest mackerel for tomorrow?'

'O.K., Dragon. Will do. Enjoy your bacon and eggs. *Bon appétit*! as they say in France.'

'*Bon appétit*!' repeated the dragon. 'I can guess what it means. *Bon appétit* to you and Jeff!'

He laid the plate very carefully on the edge of the quay. The bacon he picked up in his claws, dipped into the mustard and then put in his mouth. In small pieces. The dragon never (or hardly ever) gobbled his food. He always took polite little bites. This was mainly because he had no teeth of his own, only false ones which were in their long box in the suitcase. It was too much trouble to get them out to eat the bacon with. The fried eggs he just licked up with his long green tongue.

'Food for the gods,' he said to himself with a sigh. 'There's nothing like a good breakfast.'

Later on, Jeff and Maurice washed up. The dragon handed his plate to Maurice through the porthole.

'I've washed it in the harbour,' he said, 'but it's still wet.'

'I'll give it another wash all the same,' said Maurice under his breath.

'You're very fussy all of a sudden,' Jeff whispered back.

'No whispering,' said the dragon loudly. 'I have periscopic ears. If you don't like the way I wash plates, I won't wash them at all.'

'O.K., O.K.,' said Maurice, hastily. 'It's the harbour water I object to, not your method of washing.'

'Ah, that's different,' said the dragon, and he settled down to a quiet half-hour of after-breakfast meditation. Which did not prevent him from listening to the conversation going on in *Money-Spider*.

'We'd better go along to the Spider's Web again, I suppose. It's odd him not being there. He can't be closing the place altogether, surely?'

'The shop's got the usual junk in the window, and there's no FOR SALE board up, is there?'

'I don't know who'd buy it, anyway. Far more likely that he's in some trouble with the harbour police. We heard rumours last year, d'you remember, that the police were getting a bit suspicious? In fact, I think we ought not to be seen too often going along to the shop. We don't want to get mixed up in something like drugs.'

'Drugs? D'you think he might be doing a bit of drug-peddling?'

'Can't say. He's a crook, isn't he? Might be peddling anything.'

Then the dragon heard Maurice say: 'Look, you ought to be careful. You never know who's about and sound carries across water.'

Jeff's answer to this was a rather disgruntled remark: 'I'm a bit sick of this lark anyway. It was fun last year but now it's different –'

'You don't have to do it,' interrupted Maurice. 'I thought you loved sailing so much.'

'I do, but we're not exactly here for the sailing, are we?'

'Good heavens! We spent most of yesterday sailing, and a few days ago we brought the boat over from France. Really, Jeff, you're being a bit stupid.'

'Look, Maurice, it's very nice for your brother Peter, working in Paris. He's got a good job and I don't see why he wants to make more money on the side, especially when it involves people like you and me. After all, it *is* a dangerous game and I'm not sure that it's worth it.

He doesn't give us much of a share in the profits, does he?'

'Well, don't do it, then. I can find someone else.'

'I'm not sure your dear brother Peter would like yet another person being let into the secret. It's a bit dicey –'

'For heaven's sake, keep your voice down, Jeff. You can be heard all over the quay, I should think. Perhaps it *would* be better if I got someone else, someone a bit more cooperative.'

'Look here, I don't want to chuck it, but this is the third trip we've made this year. I gave up Easter and my spring holiday and now a week of my regular summer leave, sailing backwards and forwards across the Channel. It's getting boring. I'd like to sail somewhere else – Dartmouth, Burnham, Scotland, – there are so many places.'

'Well, in that case, why don't you find yourself a yacht that'll take you to those places as a crew? Though you're not all that hot as a sailor. I think Peter gives us quite a decent cut of the profits, and it's his boat, anyway. And we get a bit of racing and a damn good holiday out of it. But you don't *have* to come.'

'O.K. O.K. I won't open my mouth again. I'm going ashore. I want some cigarettes.'

The dragon felt Jeff's shoes trampling over his back. He was thoughtful. Something odd was going on. *Money-Spider* was not just engaged on pleasure. But what *were* these two young men up to? And brother Peter? Where did he fit in?

'I say! I say!' cried a high-pitched voice. The dragon turned his head and there was Adam on the quay, his curly hair on end, a skateboard swinging from one hand and a coke bottle clasped in the other.

'Well, say on, Adam,' said the dragon. 'I hope it's interesting, that's all, because you're interrupting a most interesting train of thought.'

'Train?' exclaimed Adam, looking down the railway track. 'I don't see any train, Dragon! Ha! Ha!'

'Ho! Ho!' replied the dragon without smiling.

'But look – talk of trains – and here it comes!' cried Adam as the diesel engine uttered a hoarse shriek under the Town Bridge, and rolled slowly towards them. As it rumbled past, the dragon said:

'You haven't actually told me anything, Adam. Your "I say! I say!" sounded as if you'd got some exciting news.'

'Not exactly,' said Adam, taking a long pull at his coke bottle. 'It was just another riddle I was going to ask you.'

'Oh,' said the dragon gloomily. 'What is it this time?'

'I say! I say! Why do –'

'Is this part of the riddle?' interrupted the dragon.

'Well, it's the way you often start a riddle,' explained Adam.

The dragon sighed heavily and a ripple fanned out right across the harbour, rocking the nearby boats. 'Well?' he asked.

'I say! I say! Why do bees hum?'

'I know nothing whatever about bees and I don't intend to find out anything. I do not care for bees,' said the dragon.

'Oh, please!' begged Adam. 'Do just ask me – why do they hum?'

'All right. Why do bees hum?'

'They don't know the words.'

The dragon was silent for a moment. Then he said: 'Adam, just come a bit nearer. I don't want anyone to hear what I'm saying.'

'Why, is it very secret?'

'Very. You see this yacht alongside me?'

'*Money-Spider*?'

'Yes. There's two young men on board called Maurice and Jeff. Something odd's going on. I often overhear them talking. They've got *something* in the yacht, and they keep saying she's "loaded". Here's a riddle for you: when is a spider not a spider?'

'When it's a *Money-Spider*.'

'No, ha! ha!'

'When it's a green dragon.'

'Of course not!'

'O.K. I give up.'

'When it's loaded.'

'I don't see it,' said Adam. 'It's not a gun, anyway. I don't think much of that as a riddle.'

63

'It's real, which is more than your riddles are,' said the dragon, annoyed.

At this moment, John came along the quay.

'What are you two talking about?' he asked, going on: 'By the way, here's some more Daddy's Sauce. A fairly full bottle.'

'He keeps saying *Money-Spider* is loaded,' said Adam to his brother. 'Whatever that means.'

'Well, I should think it means that they're smuggling something,' said John, squatting down and speaking softly into the four ears beside him.

'That's exactly what I was going to say,' said the dragon.

'What else have you heard?' asked John.

'Not much else, except that they're forever talking about going along to some shop called the Spider's Web,' explained the dragon, 'and they're annoyed and worried because it's been shut.'

'Oh, we know the Spider's Web, don't we, Adam? It's a junk-shop, down near the Ferry Office. Adam and I bought an old telescope there last year, and the glass fell out and cracked almost at once and he wouldn't take it back. He's mean. Nasty-looking. Gives me the creeps.'

'Adam and John,' began the dragon solemnly. 'We're going to do a bit of detective work. Let's all keep our eyes and ears open. There's *some* connection between your junk-shop and the yacht *Money-Spider*, and we're going to find out what.'

'O.K.,' agreed the two boys. 'Be seeing you, Dragon!' they called out as they went off down the quay.

5

Dragon Detective

'WE forgot to show you the mat we bought yesterday,' said Maurice, the next morning. He held it up – a green bathmat with the word HIS in the centre in black letters. 'We couldn't get a doormat, so we hope you don't mind a bathmat.'

The dragon was delighted with it and spread it across his central back spikes at once, continually turning round to admire it. Then he rolled over onto his back and spread the mat over his stomach. 'It looks splendid either way,' he said to himself. Breakfast was over. Maurice had gone ashore earlier to buy some mackerel on the quay – two each for himself and Jeff and four for the dragon. They were delicious and the bones were no trouble to the dragon. He just crunched them up, having put in his teeth specially for the purpose. He then washed his teeth in the harbour and dried them on a seaweed handkerchief, before putting them back in their box in the suitcase.

The two young men were lounging on the deck in the morning sunshine after breakfast, and the harbour was bustling with craft of all sizes and descriptions, most of them leaving their moorings, or being made ready for a long day's sailing. Some of the bigger yachts were making their stately way down the harbour under their engines, sails still furled. Smaller boats were gliding past, their outboard motors pop-pop-popping, while one or two of the crew hauled up the sails, and as the wind caught them and filled the flapping canvas, there were shouts of 'Shut the engine off, Bert!' and 'O.K., we're off!'

Most of the sailing dinghies were already under sail and weaving swiftly in and out between the larger craft like seagulls. They tacked up the harbour from side to side in the stiff breeze, swinging about so fast at the end of each tack that their owners had to fling themselves across and lean out backwards from the gunwale to balance their boats as they caught the wind and heeled right over. Red sails, white sails, bright blue sails – it was an enthralling sight to the dragon. The sea had always been a part of his life, for he had never lived far away from it. A harbour and its busy life, however, *was* new to him. So he lay at his mooring, listening happily to the shouts of 'Have a good day!' and 'How long are you here?' and 'Nice to see you – meet you for a drink tonight!' For the moment he had forgotten his plan to do some detective work. However, he was soon reminded of it.

The two young men on *Money-Spider* began talking in low voices to each other as they lay in the sun, and they didn't sound very happy.

'I wish we could get away,' Jeff complained gloomily, as he had done only the day before. 'Stuck here like this. And it's a marvellous day. Oh, yes, I know we sailed the day before yesterday, but I'd hoped that we'd join in one or two of the races today. We're missing everything.'

Maurice said nothing for a few minutes. 'We can't race,' he said, at last. 'You know that well enough. Why can't you shut up about it?'

'O.K., O.K.,' agreed Jeff, with a sigh. 'I take your point. Maybe Spicer will be back today and we can get rid of the stuff. We could race tomorrow then.'

'There's no need to tell the whole of Weymouth, is there?' snarled Maurice, in anger. 'You're being a right idiot, Jeff, mentioning names like that. Those boys might be just coming up to speak to the dragon, not to mention the dragon himself hearing us. Keep your mouth shut, for heaven's sake.'

'Oho!' thought the dragon, pricking up his ears. 'So they don't want me to hear their conversation, don't they? They don't know how sharp my ears are.'

'No harm in talking about racing, is there?' demanded Jeff in aggrieved tones. 'What's the main race tomorrow?'

'The Poxwell Cup, I think.'

'Well, why don't we go round to the Club and get ourselves on the list for it, at any rate, even if we do have to scratch tomorrow?'

'I suppose we could,' said Maurice without enthusiasm.

'Oh, for Pete's sake!' exploded Jeff. 'You're so gloomy, Maurice. It's like sailing in perpetual rain and fog.'

'I'm worried. That's what. You don't seem –'

'O.K., you're worried. So am I worried. Something queer's going on. That fellow Spicer –'

'Shut up, Jeff!' shouted Maurice, exasperated at his friend's stupidity.

'Oh, sorry!' exclaimed Jeff. 'Look, I'll make some more coffee and then we'll go ashore and – you know what. He might be back today.'

'We've run out of coffee,' observed Maurice. 'And milk.'

'All right!' retorted Jeff. 'It's not the end of the world, is it? I could make tea, anyway.'

'I hate tea,' complained Maurice, 'and I've run out of cigarettes. You got any, Jeff?'

'One or two, I think. Here you are.' Jeff tossed him one. As Maurice cupped his hands to light a match, Jeff went on: 'If Spicer's not there, oughtn't we to look for some other man to – er – to unload the stuff on?'

'I don't think that's a very bright suggestion,' answered Maurice. 'To start with, we don't know anyone else and we shouldn't have a clue who to go to. My brother's always dealt with Spi – this fellow, and the only reason *he* takes it is because Peter did him a good turn once and got him out of some trouble.'

'Well, yes, I see your point,' said Jeff. 'But in a place like Weymouth, I bet there *are* people willing to act as –'

'Keep your voice down,' warned Maurice, and the dragon lost the next two or three sentences till Maurice himself raised his voice to say, irritably: 'It'd only end in someone like that splitting on us to the police.'

So it was a police matter, was it? The dragon felt worried. He liked Jeff and Maurice and didn't want to see them in trouble with the law. But he was beginning to understand what the trouble was, and Maurice's next sentence made him even more certain.

'We'll try him once more,' Maurice was saying, 'and if it's no good, we shall have to think of another plan. We just can't keep the stuff aboard any longer.'

'Let's have coffee at the Mary-Rose as we've run out,' suggested Jeff.

'O.K., and there must be a bit of shopping to do. More

cigarettes for a start. Here, I'll make a list. Coffee, milk, cigarettes –'

'Bread,' contributed Jeff, 'and something for lunch if we're staying on the boat.'

'Pork pies and salad? Oh, no, let's have a pub lunch. Come on, Jeff. We'd better get weaving. I'm dying for some coffee.'

They crossed over the dragon's stomach and went off up the quay in the direction of the Mary-Rose café.

About half an hour later, Adam and John arrived. John handed the dragon another bottle of Daddy's Sauce. The dragon held it up to the light.

'Lovely!' he exclaimed. 'Nearly half full.'

'Mrs Simmonds was a bit shirty about it, actually,' said John. 'I'm wondering whether she'll produce another bottle for our table.'

'Oh, dear!' said the dragon. 'I wouldn't want you and your dear parents to go without.'

'Dear parents!' snorted Adam. 'You haven't met them.'

'Oh, go on, Adam!' protested John. 'As parents go, they're not too bad.'

'When I was a cub,' said the dragon, pursing his long mouth rather primly and looking down his nose, 'we'd never have made remarks like that about our parents. I can't think what my Aunt Dracula would say if she heard you, but perhaps she's used to these modern manners.'

'Who's your Aunt Dracula?' asked Adam.

'A very remarkable dragon. She lives at Longleat

House, where she is working at a book,' answered the dragon. 'It's a study of the behaviour of human beings. In several volumes, I believe.'

Adam burst out laughing.

'Adam,' said the dragon severely. 'What is so funny about my Aunt Dracula studying human beings? Thousands of humans study animal behaviour and very silly they often are about it.'

John felt that the dragon was annoyed, so he said hastily: 'I think we need something to liven us up. I'll go and get us cokes or ices or something.'

So he went off to a shop near the quay and came back with two custard tarts for the dragon, an ice-cream cornet for Adam and a coke for himself, and they ate and drank their elevenses slowly and lazily in the hot sun.

The dragon's thoughts had returned to the *Money-Spider* mystery. He decided, as he licked the custard off his claws, that he'd go up to Spicer's junk-shop and take a good look round it, to see if he could pick up any clues. He wanted to do this on his own, so he was quite pleased when the boys started to go, and quite annoyed when they turned back and called out: 'Have you heard the news about Sybil?'

'What news?' asked the dragon, his mind revolving round the junk-shop.

'She's disappeared,' said John, and the dragon suddenly realized that he didn't want the mackerel-coloured cat to disappear. She was part of the quay, part of Weymouth. He had often seen her since she first came to inspect him. He abandoned detection and asked John how he knew.

'They've got a notice up in the window of the Mary-

Rose café,' he said. 'It says Sybil has been missing for two days, and they're offering a reward of ten pounds for her.'

'We're going to carry out a search,' said Adam. 'Right round the harbour. She must be somewhere.'

'Good idea!' said the dragon, sorry about Sybil, but relieved that the boys were at last going.

Adam couldn't resist running back to ask him a riddle.

'Quite an easy one today, Dragon,' he said. 'What flies all day and never gets there?'

The dragon shut his mouth firmly and glared at Adam. His mind was on other things.

'Oh, come on, Dragon!' pleaded Adam.

John was impatient and already almost out of earshot. Adam called out: 'Oh, do wait for me, John!'

'If I wait for that dragon to answer the riddle, I'll be here all morning,' shouted John.

'There's no need to wait,' bellowed the dragon angrily. 'The answer to your brother's stupid riddle is – a flag. I knew that one, see?'

'Oh, fine!' cried Adam. 'See you later!' and he dashed off after John.

At last the dragon was alone. 'Sherlock Dragon,' he pondered. 'Or perhaps Dragon Holmes.' He liked the sound of that. Yes, he'd become known as Dragon Holmes when he'd solved the *Money-Spider* mystery. There were a few people wandering about the quay, but not many; it was getting on for twelve o'clock, and most families were beginning to think about lunch. The dragon also thought of it and was tempted to go into the Mary-Rose Café.

'But no,' he said sternly to himself. 'Detectives must be

prepared to go without food for days.' He paused. 'Or at least for *hours*,' he added hastily, and started to pad up the quay towards the Channel boats.

He found the junk-shop easily enough. It was not strictly speaking on the quay, but one of a small row of houses in a narrow street at right angles to it. It was a shabby little shop, the paint on its woodwork mostly peeled off. Across the board above the window was painted:

THE SPIDER'S WEB
G. Spicer – Goods Bought and Sold.

The dragon first peered through the dirty window. The goods displayed didn't look particularly interesting or valuable. There were some large shells, several green glass floats that fishermen used to tie to their nets, some murky oil paintings in chipped gilt frames and a ship's brass clock with a label which said: 'Antique. Not in working order.' The dragon didn't think much of anything, especially the pictures. 'Could paint better myself,' he commented under his breath. Then he looked through the glass panel of the door. He could see a few pieces of furniture, a copper coal-scuttle, and a table covered with pieces of china. Everything was thick with dust, a stuffed otter in a glass case looked as if it had mange, and a stuffed fish had lost its tail and gazed mournfully from its glass case in the corner of the window.

'Junk's the word,' said the dragon to himself. 'No one could make much money out of selling any of this rubbish. So, Dragon Holmes, how does Mr Spicer make his living? Elementary, my dear Watson. He buys really valuable stuff – could it be . . . brandy? – from lads like

Maurice and Jeff, and sells it I'm not sure where or how, but I'll find out, Watson. I'll find out.'

Rather pleased with himself, the dragon left the shop window and inspected the small row of houses. Most of them were rather down-at-heel. On one side of the Spider's Web was a marine store where fishing tackle and such things were sold. On the other was an empty shop that had once been a café. Its windows were boarded up and several of the roof tiles were missing. The dragon went round to the alley running along behind the houses, and discovered that each one had a small back-yard. The Spider's Web had a strong, new-looking door to its yard, with a heavy padlock. The empty house had suffered from vandalism. The door of its yard had been almost torn off its hinges. Inside was a variety of unwanted objects – a rusty pram, a mattress with most of the stuffing coming out of it, and several worn-out motor tyres. The dragon looked quickly up and down the alley. Nobody was in sight. He went into the yard of the empty house and pushed the door as shut as he could on its one remaining hinge. He then stood on his back legs and peered over into the yard of The Spider's Web.

There was something standing in it, against the wall, covered with a black tarpaulin. The dragon shifted and had another look from a different angle. No doubt about it. It was a motor-bicycle. The front wheel was sticking out from under the tarpaulin and the paint on its mudguard looked shiny and new.

'Well now,' thought Dragon Holmes. 'Just what do we make of this, Watson? If his bike is here, he can't be away on it, can he? Therefore he is probably somewhere about in Weymouth, or very near it. And he values that bike.' The dragon could see that it was chained to a drainpipe. Also there was the new and solid yard door with its heavy padlock. 'But he wouldn't go to all this trouble just for a motor-bike, would he, Watson?' went on the dragon. 'In which case, there must be more valuable objects in his shop than moth-eaten stuffed otters and bad oil paintings and ship's clocks that don't work.'

At this moment, he heard the sound of a car pulling up, it seemed at the front of the shop, and almost immediately the much louder sound of a car coming along the alley. He hastily ducked in case he was seen, but not before he had spotted on the car roof the blue lamp of a police car. Peering with one eye through the partly-open yard door, he saw that the police car had stopped in the alley, just behind Spicer's yard. 'Covering the back entrance, in case he tries to get out that way,' thought the dragon, who was rather amazed at the way he had become a detective and how his mind slipped naturally into detective-like thoughts. But his immediate problem was how to get out of the yard. It was no good hoping that the police wouldn't see him. He was not a cat that might slip out unobserved. No, he must do things the other way round. He walked boldly out into the alley, making a fair amount of noise as he pushed through the creaking door. Two policemen were getting out of the car and the dragon turned quickly to them, and cried, before they could ask questions:

'Splendid! The police – just the people I wanted to see!'

'What exactly are you –' began one of the policemen, but the dragon interrupted him with a wave of the paw.

'Just keep on the watch here,' he said. 'If Spicer's

inside, this is how he'll try to get away. And I strongly advise you to have a look at what's standing in Spicer's yard.' The dragon rubbed his nose with his paw in a rather knowing way, and leaving the two policemen too taken aback to protest, he hurried round the corner of the alley to the front of the little row of houses.

To his intense excitement, he saw that another police car was parked outside the Spider's Web, and that three policemen were standing round the shop door, unlocking the padlock – 'with a master key, no doubt,' said the dragon to himself. 'Useful things, master keys. I must get one if I stay on in detective work.' The policemen looked round when they saw him, and he smiled politely and said: 'Good afternoon, officers.' They had now got the door open and were about to enter the shop, when he went up close to them, and asked in a low, confidential sort of voice: 'I wonder if I can be of any assistance?'

There was a slight pause, and then the Detective-Sergeant said: 'Very kind of you I'm sure, Sir, but I think we can manage.'

'I thought I ought to tell you,' went on the dragon, looked down modestly at his right paw, 'that I've been doing a little investigating myself. You might like to know what I saw in the backyard.'

'What did you see?' asked the sergeant.

'A large and I should imagine a powerful motor-bicycle,' replied the dragon. 'Underneath a tarpaulin and presumably belonging to our friend Spicer. From which I deduce that he can't be far away.'

The sergeant said: 'Thanks. We've got a couple of men round the back. No doubt they –'

'Yes, I told them about the motor-bike,' said the dragon.

'Oh, you did? You should join the force, Sir.' The Sergeant smiled kindly at the dragon, who promptly cut in with: 'Of course, it might be just that he *has* gone away and left the motor-bike behind.'

The Sergeant showed signs of having had enough, and was turning away to enter the house when the dragon suddenly remembered something. During the night there had been some heavy rain. In fact, it had woken him up, and he had had to put on his woolly hat to keep it off his head. In the early morning, it had cleared away, but of one thing the dragon was quite certain. There was not a sign of rain on the tarpaulin that covered the motor-bike.

He laid his paw on the Sergeant's sleeve and said: 'Just a minute, Sergeant. I've thought of something.'

The Sergeant looked impatient. 'Well?' he asked. No 'Sir' this time.

'It might be rather important,' said the dragon. 'There is no rain whatever on the black tarpaulin covering Spicer's bike. Not a trace, not even in the folds.'

'Now that *is* an interesting bit of information,' said the Sergeant, looking better pleased. 'Hawkins, go round and see if the other two are in the yard.'

'It's heavily padlocked,' observed the dragon.

'How did *you* see the bike then, Sir?'

'I went into the next door yard,' answered the dragon. 'It was open, and I went in and looked over the wall.'

'Well, I'm blessed. You're a bit of a detective, aren't you, Sir?'

'A little hobby of mine,' said the dragon. 'Anything I can do to help you, just call me in. I'm moored near the Jolly Sailor.'

'Thanks very much, Sir. I'll remember,' said the Sergeant, and went into the shop.

The dragon walked quickly across the quay, climbed down some stone steps, and launched himself into the water to swim up the harbour to his berth. He felt exhausted with excitement; but more was to come.

6

Enter a Parrot

THE two old sailors who often sat on a stone bench outside the Jolly Sailor pub, or stood on the quayside, leaning on a rail, were there today. There was a kind of magic about the two Leaners. Somehow you never saw them walking along the quay to their favourite haunt. One minute they weren't there. The next minute, they were. They were so much a part of the harbour scene that they might have been a pair of bollards or a couple of capstans.

As the dragon tied up his mooring rope, he heard Bill Pouncy say, first taking his empty pipe out of his mouth: 'I'll need some baccy come dinnertime.'

'You want a fill o'mine?' asked George Snook, his companion with the three teeth like tombstones.

'Thank 'ee, no. I like me own better.'

The two companions then fell silent again. Their calm blue eyes scanned the harbour slowly and restfully, and had a calming effect upon the dragon. After a few minutes he asked them if they'd seen Adam and John.

'Not to say *seen* them,' said George, 'though I thought I'd heard their voices this morning.'

There was another long pause and then Bill Pouncy said: 'Nice pair of boys, them two.'

As the conversation seemed to have got started, the dragon blew a lazy puff of smoke in the direction of the two old men and said slowly and thoughtfully, as if he'd been considering the question for an hour or more: 'Have you known the boys for a long time?'

'They been here the last two-three years, ain't it?' asked George.

'Aye, this must be their third summer here,' agreed Bill. 'They always stay at Mrs Simmonds' up the quay.'

'The lady who keeps a good supply of Daddy's Sauce,' observed the dragon, licking his lips.

'Daddy's Sauce? Why –'

'Never mind,' said the dragon hastily. 'It's a little arrangement I have with the boys.'

'She's a good cook, that Mrs Simmonds,' remarked Bill.

'Good cooks,' murmured the dragon dreamily, catching the slow manner of speech from the Leaners. 'Good cooks are worth their weight in gold.'

'My mother, God rest her soul, was a queen o' cooks,' observed Bill. 'She died thirty year ago, and I haven't never tasted a real good steak and kidney pudden since.'

'Very sad for you,' said the dragon, shaking his

head mournfully. 'Now, I don't cook much myself. I eat what people leave behind, usually in paper bags, and I can always tell whose wife is a good cook, and whose isn't. It's the pastry that gives her away – I can smell the difference between a shop sausage roll and a home-made one at a distance of ten yards.'

'Ah,' said Bill with a heavy sigh. 'If all the wives were good cooks, the world'd be a happier place.'

'It would, it would,' agreed the dragon. 'Now my friend, the mermaid –'

'The lass who lives in Kynance Cove?' interposed George.

'That's the one,' answered the dragon. 'She can cook a real treat. And sew. She's like the girl in the song,' and with this the dragon lifted up his voice and warbled a verse of the sea-shanty, Billy-Boy.

> *'Can she cook a bit o' steak, Billy Boy, Billy Boy?*
> *Can she cook a bit o' steak, me Billy Boy?*
>> *She can cook a bit o' steak,*
>> *Aye, and make a girdle cake,*
>> *And me Nancy kittled me fancy, Oh,*
>> *Me charming Billy Boy!'*

'You're quite a singer, ain't you, Dragon?' said Bill, admiringly. 'You ought to join us in the Jolly Sailor of an evening. We often have a bit of a singsong there.'

'I couldn't get into the bar,' said the dragon, sadly. 'I'm too big.'

The Leaners looked up and down the dragon's length and then nodded their heads, murmuring: 'Much too big.'

After another long, peaceful silence, Bill said: 'You know that parrot you wanted? We think we've found one for you.'

'Whyever didn't you –' began the dragon eagerly and then reminded himself that you mustn't hurry Leaners. So he waited. George spoke next, after very slowly relighting his pipe – the match blew out four times – while the dragon clenched and unclenched his jaws with excitement, and little trickles of green smoke seeped out of his long mouth.

'He's a grey African parrot,' Bill went on.

'With a red tail?'

'With a red tail.'

'When can I see him?'

'Ought to be here any moment now,' said George. 'It's getting on for twelve o'clock. Any minute now Ralph Pearce oughter be here. Pub's open, and he'll want a drink. He's a Portland man and Portland's a dusty, dry little old island, where folks do need a drop of drink or their throats get closed right up with stone-dust.'

'How unpleasant!' exclaimed the dragon. 'Why ever don't they do something about it?' The dragon liked to be practical.

Both old men turned and gazed at him in silence, until the dragon felt quite uncomfortable. At last George said: 'It's always been that way on Portland.'

The dragon felt there was nothing more to be said about Portland, so he returned to the parrot.

'Why is this person selling the parrot?' he asked, for he didn't intend to buy some bald old bird, or a cross-tempered creature who'd bite.

'His missus don't like the bird,' said George.

'It's the bird as don't like the missus,' corrected Bill. 'Speak of the devil – here he comes!'

An old van had drawn up outside the Jolly Sailor, a faded blue Morris. Out came a tall, lean, bearded man, wearing blue denims and a fisherman's navy-blue smock with wide pockets. A peaked cap was stuck jauntily on the back of his brown curly hair.

'Morning to you!' he called out, as he walked across the railway track towards the Leaners.

'This here's the dragon what's interested in your parrot,' said Bill, and the bearded man walked to the edge of the quay and looked down at the dragon. 'Pleased to meet you,' he said, and held out a strong, very brown hand.

'Me too,' said the dragon, giving him a green paw.

'My, you're a fine fellow!' exclaimed the bearded one. 'Twenty-five to thirty feet if you're an inch. How d'you come to be here in Weymouth, Dragon?'

'Just on holiday,' answered the dragon simply. 'I sailed here. Up the Channel from Plymouth Ho! Ho!'

'Is that what they call it now?' asked the newcomer. 'As far as I remember it was just one "Ho" but things change. That's life.'

One of the nicest things about sailors is that they don't argue and are never surprised at anything.

'My name's Ralph Pearce, from Portland,' said the curly-haired man. 'I've had this parrot for several years. Name of Jacko.'

'Jacko!' repeated the dragon. 'I like that for a name. Where is he?'

'He's in the van,' said Ralph. 'I see you've got a cage and a very nice one. You'll need a cover for him at night.

I'll give you the green baize cover my wife made for
him – if you buy him, that is.'

'Can I see him?' asked the dragon, very excited.

'Why not? I've brought him for you to look at,' and
with that, Ralph Pearce walked back to his van and
opened it. He brought out a big cage, and inside it was a
grey African parrot with a red tail. Ralph carried him
over in his cage and set it down on the edge of the quay.
Jacko looked at the dragon with black, beady eyes, as if
he was thinking of buying the dragon, not the other way
round. He then screwed his head round almost from back
to front and said:

'Clever Jacko! Here we go!' With which he swung himself upside down on his perch.

'He's a fine bird!' cried the dragon delighted. 'What else can he say?'

'Oh, quite a number of things. Give him time and he'll bring 'em all out for you. And he whistles a lot. Very tuneful this bird is; ain't you, Jacko?'

The parrot, now upright again, polished his black beak vigorously on his wooden perch and said in brisk, matter-of-fact tones: 'How are you today?'

'Very well, thank you,' replied the dragon, beaming with pleasure.

'We'll go and have a drink in the Jolly Sailor,' said Ralph, 'just to give you time to get acquainted with him, and to make up your mind whether you want him.'

'You haven't said how much I'm to pay for him,' said the dragon.

'Nor I have. Would five pounds be too much?'

'It's a lot,' said the dragon, looking very gloomy. 'You see, I don't have much money, only what I pick up on the sands and rocks down in Cornwall.'

'Well, you think about the parrot,' said Ralph, 'and I'll think about the price. Can we bring you anything from the pub, Dragon?'

'You could. A pint of light ale and two or three ham sandwiches. Better be three. Or four.'

'Right, that'll be on me,' said Ralph, and he and the two Leaners walked across to the Jolly Sailor.

The Jolly Sailor stood on a corner where a side street came out on to the quay at right angles. It was painted a greenish-brown colour – a cool colour for sunny days and yet a warm colour for cold ones. It was a very friendly pub and had a large number of regular customers, apart from scores of visitors in the summer season.

Jacko watched the three men walk across to the Jolly Sailor, then he amused himself by climbing up the side of his cage with his grey, knotty feet. Once at the top, he swung himself over and hung upside down for several minutes, looking around him, especially at the dragon, in a quizzical way. The dragon thought how strange it must be to see the world upside down, and wondered whether it looked better or worse that way up. Then he decided that if the parrot was to be his companion in his lonely Cornish cave, he must get to know the bird. Resting his head on the quay, level with the cage, he said in a low, friendly voice: 'Hullo, Polly! Jacko, my boy! Hullo to you! How d'you like the harbour, Jacko? Does it look nice upside down?'

Jacko stared at the dragon for a few seconds, then he uttered a loud squawk, hung onto the top bar of his cage with one foot, folded the other foot up underneath him and proceeded to swivel rapidly from right to left, whistling melodiously as he turned to and fro.

It made the dragon quite giddy to see him but he felt he must make another effort to talk to the parrot, so he said: 'C'mon, Jacko, say something. What d'you think of this?' and he blew a green smoke ring which travelled slowly up the side of the cage, then over the top, and finally faded into nothing. Jacko watched it and when it vanished, he shrieked: 'Happy birthday to you!' several times over. This did not seem to the dragon to have much connection with his green smoke ring. Having noticed that the parrot ended his birthday song with the words 'Happy birthday, dear Jacko,' the dragon thought he'd teach him something different, and sang: 'Happy birthday, dear *dragon*!' 'Happy birthday, dear Jacko!' shrieked the parrot.

'Come on,' urged the dragon. 'Say: "Happy birthday, dear *dragon*!" Just try, Jacko!' But no amount of repetition had any effect. Jacko fell silent. He climbed down to his perch, folded one leg underneath him and closed his eyes.

'I'll have to be patient,' said the dragon to himself. 'Also, he hasn't much birdseed. Perhaps he's hungry. Ah, there come John and Adam. They can go and buy me some.'

The boys were running down the quay. Adam's fair hair was standing on end and he was panting like a grampus. His red-haired brother John was a fast runner and stopped at last, to let Adam catch up with him. Just at that moment, a police car came past them, lights flashing, and, to the dragon's astonishment, both boys waved cheerfully to the men sitting in it, and the officer beside the driver actually saluted and grinned. It was the Sergeant whom the dragon had spoken to outside the Spider's Web, and the dragon gripped the edge of the quay with his front paws and pulled himself up as high as he could, hoping that the Sergeant would see him and wave to *him*. Sure enough, the next moment, the car was level with him. Luckily the tide was in, so a lot of the dragon appeared over the edge of the quay. The car slowed down and the Sergeant leaned out of his window and cried: 'Many thanks, Sir. Very useful information you gave us.'

'Any time I can be of service,' answered the dragon and wished that he had a peaked cap that he could put his paw to in a salute. Instead, he blew a puff of green smoke towards the departing police car.

The boys half ran the rest of the way to the dragon's mooring. Then they squatted down by the parrot-cage, breathing hard and speaking in low voices.

'I say, I say, Dragon,' began Adam.

'I hope this isn't another long riddle,' the dragon interrupted quickly. 'I want you to go and buy me some parrot-food as soon as possible.' He ferreted in his ear for his purse.

'Never mind the parrot-food,' said John. 'This is much more important, but first – tell us – how d'you come to know that police Sergeant? *What* was he saying to you? We couldn't hear?'

'Never mind,' answered the dragon. 'You tell me your news first. Why did he wave and salute you, any-way?'

'We've been helping the police,' said Adam, 'and we know the secret behind that junk-shop.'

'The Spider's Web?' asked the dragon, pretending he knew nothing about it.

'The one that's been shut for ages,' said John.

'Yes, I've heard those two lads on *Money-Spider* complaining it's always shut. I suppose you didn't see them there today, did you?' asked the dragon.

'That's just it,' said John. 'We *did* see them there. We were quite a long way down the quay when we saw the police car in front of the shop –'

'So we dashed along to see what was happening,' interrupted Adam, 'and at that moment, Jeff and Maurice came round the corner near the shop, and ran straight into the police, and Jeff said: "Oh, it's open at last –"'

'And Maurice nearly hit him for making such a stupid remark,' went on John. 'The Sergeant said: "Were you looking for Mr Spicer?" And Maurice grabbed Jeff by the arm before he could say anything else and it looked as if they were going to make a dash for it, but –'

'But the policeman caught up with them,' interrupted Adam.

'Caught up with them?' repeated the dragon. 'He didn't arrest them, did he?'

'Here we go again!' warbled Jacko, suddenly, in a melodious voice, and added: 'La-di-da-di-da!'

'Shut up, Jacko!' ordered the dragon. Jacko had caught the atmosphere of excitement and danced up and down on his perch squawking and whistling and repeating some of his catch phrases while the boys went on talking.

'He didn't arrest them,' explained John. 'But he stopped them and asked if they'd wanted to buy something at the shop.'

'And then we came up,' said Adam, 'and they asked us, too.'

'What did Jeff and Maurice say?'

'They just said they wanted to know the price of a ship's clock in the window. And the police asked if they were friends of Mr Spicer's, because they'd been seen at the shop more than once, and Maurice jabbed his elbow into Jeff –'

'I saw him!' cried Adam.

'Because Jeff was opening his mouth to say something and Maurice cut in loudly, saying they didn't know Mr Spicer. Not personally. They were just interested in the clock.'

'The clock was out of order, anyway,' murmured the

dragon, almost to himself, but was quickly aroused by John saying: 'How d'you know?'

'I'll tell you in a minute,' said the dragon hastily. 'Go on.'

'Well then *we* said,' began Adam. 'Shut up! It's my turn to tell him, John.'

'O.K. then,' said John.

'*We* said that we'd bought a telescope there last year and we wanted to ask the man if he'd mend it free of charge, 'cos the glass kept dropping out, and we'd paid for it with some birthday money and it was jolly annoying, like losing a birthday present almost before you've opened it.'

'Oh, you do go on,' exlaimed his brother. 'Cut it short, man.'

But as Adam started to speak again, Jacko shrieked: 'Never say die! Never say die! La-di-da-di-da!'

'You be quiet!' ordered the dragon. 'Go on! This is terribly exciting. I want to know what happened next.'

John took up the story. 'Well, by this time several policemen had got out of the two police cars. Maurice and Jeff didn't seem to want to stay. I don't know where they went, but suddenly I looked round and they weren't there. We hung about for a bit, and the policemen came out of the shop with some cardboard boxes and two or three wooden packing-cases, and one of the police cars was a sort of van and they shoved all the stuff inside. And I went up and asked if they'd found Mr Spicer and what about our telescope? You tell the dragon what he said, Adam.'

'Well, he said no, we haven't found him, sonny. I do hate being called sonny. And then –'

'Then he added: "But he'll turn up," and he grinned at us,' said John. 'So I asked him if we'd be wanted as witnesses because of our telescope, but he said probably not. At the moment they weren't needing witnesses, and anyway it wasn't telescopes they were interested in. They locked up the shop again and got into the police cars and drove away.'

> 'Half a pound of tuppenny rice,
> Half a pound of treacle!'

sang the parrot, and then suddenly flinging himself upside down on his perch he went on:

> 'That's the way the money all goes,
> Pop goes the weasel!'

Jacko then laughed so raucously that the dragon sternly covered up his cage in the green baize cloth. Then he asked the boys if there was any more to the story.

'Not exactly,' said John, 'but I'll tell you what. I think I know what Mr Spicer is. He's a fence.'

'A fence?' queried the dragon. And cocking an eye at Adam, he smiled blandly and said: 'Here's a riddle for you, Adam. When is a fence not a fence?'

'I know the answer! It's when it's a man who buys and sells stolen goods.'

'Or contraband goods,' added John. 'Things like whisky and brandy and tobacco and watches. I think "fence" is a slang word that thieves use. Now tell us how you were mixed up with the police, Dragon.'

'I was not exactly "mixed up" with the police,' said the dragon. 'I was able to give them some useful information that I had found out during – er – some detection work I'd carried out.'

'You've been doing detective work?' exclaimed Adam, and afraid that he might offend the dragon by sounding so disbelieving, John gave his brother a kick, and cut in quickly with: 'I bet you'd make a first-class detective, Dragon. A real Sherlock Holmes.'

The dragon was so pleased at this speech that he could hardly say a word, and only after the boys had said 'Come on! Out with it!' and 'We can't wait!' and similar encouraging remarks, could he get on with the story of his visit to the Spider's Web, and the find he had made in its yard.

Just as he was finishing the account of his exploits, he noticed that Jeff and Maurice had come along the quay behind them, and were standing together near the parrot's cage. They were obviously listening to what they could hear of the conversation, and the dragon wondered how long they had been there. Maurice whispered something to Jeff. Both of them looked nervous and very down in the mouth. When they realized that they had been seen, Jeff came up to the dragon and said, pointing to the cage: 'What's this you've got?'

'It's my parrot,' explained the dragon. 'Well, actually, he's not mine yet because I haven't paid for him, but he will be mine, I hope. I've always wanted one and I brought my parrot-cage with me to Weymouth, in case I found one. Ah, here they are!' He pointed with his paw towards the Jolly Sailor, out of which were coming the Leaners and the parrot's owner, Ralph. The latter held out a mug to the dragon, saying: 'Here's your pint, Dragon.'

Having such long jaws, the dragon couldn't drink beer or anything else like other people. He grasped the mug in his right paw, threw his head back, opened his toothless jaws and poured the beer down his yawning red throat.

'That's the stuff!' he pronounced, smacking his lips with a sound like a pistol shot.

'It's a special brew,' said Ralph. 'Nothing but the best for a dragon. How d'you feel about Jacko?'

'How much did you say I'd have to pay for him?' asked the dragon warily, hoping that Ralph might have forgotten.

'Well, I said five pounds, didn't I? Let's have another look at him.' He went up to the cage, and the others crowded round, including Jeff and Maurice. Jacko looked round at his audience with his black, beady eyes, bobbed his head up and down several times and then said clearly and loudly: 'One, two, three, four – *can* say five but I won't!'

Everyone laughed, but the dragon's laugh was a positive bellow.

'I like that!' he exclaimed. 'Oh, I really think that's wonderful!'

'It's great!' agreed the others, and Adam and John

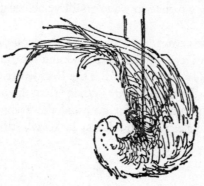

repeated the words, and the Leaners and even gloomy Maurice and Jeff joined in: 'One, two, three, four – *can* say five but I won't!'

Then they calmed down and the dragon asked Ralph: 'Suppose I give you *four* pounds? Will that be enough? I'm not rich.'

'O.K. That'll do,' said Ralph, good-naturedly. 'It sounds as if you *can* say five, but you won't!'

The dragon laughed, pulled his wallet from his left ear and extracted four one-pound notes from it. 'There!' he said. 'At last I have my African parrot, and I'm very much obliged to you for bringing him over from Portland. What about your cage?'

'Oh, yes, the cage. I don't really want it,' answered Ralph. 'As you've got such a fine one, what about giving it to Oxfam?'

So it was agreed that John and Adam would take it to the Oxfam shop that afternoon, and get some parrot-food as well. Ralph departed for Portland. The Leaners went home for their dinners, and so did the boys. The dragon was going to eat his ham sandwiches. They couldn't say any more to each other about the Spider's Web, but the dragon gave the boys an enormous wink as they turned to wave goodbye before going off up the quay.

An hour or more passed peacefully enough in the hot sun. Maurice and Jeff, after some argument, took *Money-Spider* to a boatyard in the Backwater to have the galley porthole replaced. When they had gone, the dragon closed his eyes for his usual afternoon nap. As he went off to sleep, he could hear Jacko whistling softly to himself.

7

The Dragon Finds Old Friends

IN the late afternoon, a harbour wakes up from its sleep and comes to life, with new boats coming in looking for moorings, and others coming back to their berths after a day's sailing. The dragon was drowsy and only just aware of the change, when there was a scraping sound and several bumps to his long green person. Annoyed, he opened his eyes to see a tall sailing-boat alongside, instead of *Money-Spider*, and to hear an angry voice shout:

'Hi! Why aren't your fenders out?'

There was a crunching sound and a bump or two.

'What the hell!' shouted the voice. 'You've taken half the paint off my hull!'

'Too bad!' exclaimed the dragon angrily. 'You've blunted some of my scales!'

'Well, you should have had your fenders out. I've got mine out but I can't cover every inch of the hull.'

Fenders are made usually of rope or rubber, and are hung along the side of a boat to protect it from scrapes and scratches. *Money-Spider* had plenty of fenders so the dragon had never been asked to put any along his scaly length. Anyway, he didn't know what fenders were, so he said indignantly: 'I am NOT a fireplace. I do not have fenders. Nor mantelpieces. Nor coal-scuttles. What are you talking about?'

'I'm not talking about fireplaces, you clot. FENDERS. F-E-N-'

'That's quite enough from you,' interrupted the dragon, furious at being called a clot. 'Any more of your lip and I'll *melt your mast.*'

There was a short silence. Then the voice said in a quite different tone: 'You'll do *what?*'

'You heard. I'll melt your mast, which I see is a nasty metal one. Now, we always used sound timber in the good old days. Hi, look out with that boathook. Stop prodding me. Ouch!'

The boathook had poked a soft place between his ribs. He rolled over onto his front, creating a small tidal wave which sent the boat rocking. Angrily, he blew a thick green smoke ring which encircled the end of the boathook and melted the iron hook into a small blob of iron that dropped into the water with a hiss.

'There you are! See?' cried the dragon triumphantly. 'You wouldn't like that to happen to your mast, would you?'

Whoever was holding the boathook dropped it, but

the dragon caught it neatly in his paw and handed it back. Meanwhile the crew of three were staring in dumb amazement at the green scaly back which they had so foolishly mistaken for the deck of another yacht.

'It's a . . . a . . . sea-serpent! I'll be jiggered if it isn't!'

'Save yourselves trouble,' said the dragon coldly. 'I am R. Dragon. And if you want to walk over me to get to the quay, you may, only be quick about it.'

'What about this paint you've scraped off our hull?' asked a man's voice in a surly tone.

'Denis – shut up! It's a dragon,' said the girl. 'You don't want to quarrel with it. It might eat you.'

'If you want to be nasty,' said the dragon, 'let me tell you that you've definitely damaged some of my scales and I'll be sending you a bill for the repairs. When my lawyer has drawn it up.' (They weren't to know, of course, that he hadn't got a lawyer and didn't even know of one.)

'Oh, come on, Denis,' said the other man. 'Let's keep it friendly, and get ashore. I need a beer.'

'O.K.,' said Denis. 'We'll forget the paint.'

'And I'll forget the scales,' said the dragon. 'Let's be friends. Over you go.'

The two men and the girl stepped off their boat-deck onto his back and then up onto the quay. At that very moment the sun slipped out from behind a tall warehouse and sent a golden bar of light across the harbour. It caught the tips of the dragon's yellow horns, so that they shone bright gold. The trio looked admiringly at him.

'Isn't he beautiful!' exclaimed the girl.

The dragon was very pleased. He reached out, took the girl's hand in his paw and kissed it in a knightly fashion.

'Oh, I say!' she cried. 'I've never had that happen before! He's real old-fashioned. You never kiss my hand, Denis.'

'I don't think I want to try, thanks,' said Denis with a grin.

The dragon then shook hands with both of the men. They told him they were called Denis and Hugh, and the girl was Hugh's sister, Jean.

'Delighted to meet you,' said the dragon. 'No hard feelings about fenders and boathooks, I hope?'

They all said no, of course not, and then hurried across the quay to the pub. Through the door as they opened it came the sound of a piano, and voices singing an old song, a favourite of the dragon's: *Daisy, Daisy, give me your answer, do.* The pub door closed and the dragon gazed thoughtfully at it.

'Now where did I last hear *Daisy, Daisy*?' he muttered to himself under his breath.

He was still staring at the door of the Jolly Sailor when it opened again. This time the song was another old favourite: *It's a long way to Tipperary.* The singing burst out onto the salty air, accompanied on a piano that was rather out of tune and had several keys missing, but whoever was playing it had a very robust touch and kept them all going.

Suddenly the dragon remembered. He climbed quickly out onto the quay and, lifting up his voice, joined in the singing, though the words that he sang were quite different:

> *'It's a long way to Weymouth harbour,*
> *It's a long way to go!*
> *It's a long way to Weymouth harbour,*
> *And the nicest pub I know!*
> *And William's at the piano,*
> *And Fred is keeping time,*
> *It's a long, long way to Weymouth harbour,*
> *And I can't think of another rhyme!'*

The dragon fairly bellowed out the last line of his song, and the people in the Jolly Sailor's bar came tumbling out onto the quay, looking wildly about them and shouting: 'Who was that?' and 'Who was singing?' and 'Where is he?' and other exclamations of amazement. Not believing it could be the dragon's voice that they had heard, they left him standing by the pub and rushed towards the edge of the quay. One tall, thin man caught his foot in the dragon's mooring rope and fell headlong into the water, but the dragon quickly pushed the crowd aside, threw him one end of the rope and pulled him out.

'I knew it!' cried the dragon, surveying this unfortunate figure, dripping with water, his hair over his eyes, his moustaches drooping like wet string. 'It's William! I guessed it must be when I heard those songs being pounded out on the pub piano.'

'Dragon! It can't be! It is!' and the dragon felt himself clasped in William's damp embrace.

'Where's Fred?' demanded the dragon.

'Here I am!' shouted someone who was just emerging from the Jolly Sailor's door. The dragon and Fred shook both hands and paws most warmly, while William stood beside them, his long sad face looking more like a mule's with the stomach-ache than anything else. His teeth were chattering, and the poor man was standing in a pool of water.

'What William needs is a hot drink – brandy and lemon and sugar,' cried the dragon in his organizing manner. 'Just put that pewter mug down on the quay, my good friend –' he was speaking to one of the pub's customers who was just lifting a mug of beer to his lips. The gentleman put the mug down on the stone of the quay as directed, and in a kind of dazed obedience, staggered into the pub, muttering: 'Brandy and lemon! Boiling water! Lemon and boiling brandy! Dragon and lemon!'

'It's a girt dragon!' said one of the little crowd on the quay. 'What's he going to do next?'

'Reckon he'll eat us if he turns nasty,' said another.

The dragon glared at them. 'Now,' he said sternly. 'I am not one to perform parlour tricks for your amusement, but I'm going to do one for the sake of my dear old friend William. He's catching his death of cold and until that brandy and lemon appears, we'll give him the next best thing – hot ale. Watch!'

The pewter mug was just by the dragon's front paws. He leaned down and breathed a fine, curling tongue of green smoke that settled round the mug. This heated the metal, so that the beer in the mug began to steam.

'There you are!' cried the dragon, holding the mug towards William. 'Mind out! The handle's hot! Here, borrow this, William.' And he handed the shivering William a large red spotted handkerchief.

'Cor stone the crows!' cried Fred, who was standing beside William, trying to squeeze water out of his shirt.

'He's still got that red spotted handkerchief he borrowed off me years ago!'

William wound the handkerchief round the handle of the mug. Rather cautiously, he sipped a little of the steaming beer, then leant back and poured the rest of it down his throat.

'That's it!' cried the dragon, beaming upon everyone with his long toothless jaws.

A few minutes later, the hot brandy and lemon was brought out and William drank that as well. The innkeeper then came forward and having decided that he wasn't dreaming, he said to William: 'Here, you just come right in and the missus'll let you have a hot bath and some dry clothes.'

William followed the landlord into the Jolly Sailor. A few people left the gathering, but some of them, including the Leaners, stood around admiring the dragon, and listening to his conversation with Fred, which they must have found very puzzling, for it started with Fred saying:

'My word, that was some drive, weren't it? All the way from Cornwall to that place near London – what was it called?'

'St Aubyn's,' answered the dragon. 'Fancy meeting you here, Fred, after all these years. I suppose you've taken your removal van all over England by now. What are you doing here?'

'We gone up in the world,' said Fred. 'We got three vans now, and a small warehouse along the quay, where we store furniture and so on. Here, Dragon, we must celebrate our meeting again.'

'We'll have to celebrate tonight or tomorrow evening,' said the dragon, 'but we can't celebrate without William.'

One of the Leaners, Bill Pouncy, suddenly appeared from the bar door of the Jolly Sailor, carrying two tankards of beer. He pushed his way through the little knot of bystanders, saying: 'Here y'are, Dragon, a pint of the best, and for you as well, Fred.'

'He knows your name!' cried the dragon, delighted.

'Of course he does! We been in Weymouth this last three years, ain't we, Bill?'

'All good friends here,' said Bill, now joined by George Snook, who added: 'We be a kind of brotherhood of the quay.'

'Go on with you and your brotherhoods!' laughed Bill Pouncy. 'George was always one for fancy names. He's a great reader, you see. Now I – I never open a book. Waste o'time, I reckon.'

'I'm sorry to hear that,' said the dragon. 'I'd like to have given you a copy of my memoirs.'

'I won't say I *can't* read,' said Bill hastily. 'I wouldn't like you to think that.'

The dragon opened his suitcase and ferreted about in it, at last producing a book with a picture of himself on the cover.

'There you are,' he said, giving it to George Snook. 'That's my memoirs, all about my life at the court of King Arthur.'

'*The Dragon's Quest*.' George read the title slowly. 'You wrote this? Well I never! It's real kind of you to give it to me. I'll treasure it. When I've got a pen handy, you must write my name in it.'

'Of course I will,' said the dragon, taking a long

drink of the Jolly Sailor's best ale, and emptying the tankard. 'I'll certainly do that.'

'Don't I get a copy?' asked Bill, rather aggrieved.

'You said you didn't read,' put in a bystander and there was general laughter.

'I didn't say I *couldn't* read, did I?' protested Bill Pouncy.

'That's all right. No problem,' said the dragon at once. He opened his suitcase again and extracted another copy of The Dragon's Quest – he usually carried two or three to give away, as he was rather proud of his memoirs.

One or two of the crowd then started to ask for copies. The dragon looked round at them and said firmly: 'I'm not giving away any more. Only to personal friends like George and Bill. You can buy it in a book-shop.'

Fred then pushed his way to the dragon and said he'd just popped into the pub to see that William hadn't caught his death of cold.

'I should hope not!' said the dragon. 'He must be well

103

before tomorrow night, because then we're going to have –' and with this, the dragon gave a huge grin, and blew out a puff of green smoke to cries of 'Oh, look!' 'Isn't it beautiful!' 'My, he's a clever dragon!'

'Do go on, dragon,' urged Fred. 'What's going to happen tomorrow night?'

'Our celebration,' said the dragon. 'I'm going to lay on a real feast, I've decided; the Jolly Sailor will provide the drinks, and we'll have the best sing-song ever.'

'How are you going to get into the pub, Dragon?' asked Fred. 'Ain't you too big?'

'The pub's coming out to me,' said the dragon in a grand manner. 'Wait till I've talked to the man who runs it. I'll ask him to bring out a table, for the eats and drinks, and what's more – I'll persuade him to bring out the –' The dragon paused again. Everyone held his breath, there was so much excitement in the air.

'The what?' shouted Fred. 'I bet I know! It's the –' and both he and the dragon bellowed at the tops of their voices: 'THE PIANO!'

With that, the dragon started to sing: *It's a long way to Weymouth harbour* again but he broke off half-way through, to borrow another of Fred's handkerchiefs and mop his eyes.

'It's all too much for me,' confessed the dragon. 'Meeting you and William again, all this lovely beer, and all those happy memories.' And then the dragon said a rather croaky goodbye to all, wiped his eyes once more, blew a little puff of green smoke, and lowered himself into the water of the harbour. He tied up his mooring rope and closed his eyes. It had been a wonderful day.

8

Party Preparations

'THE all-important thing is the FOOD,' announced the dragon the next morning, when the boys arrived with yet another bottle of Daddy's Sauce. The dragon was so busy making lists of food for the party that he hardly gave a glance to the sauce. He was surrounded by screwed-up pieces of paper which he had thrown away.

'First of all,' he went on, 'is lots of meat pies.'

'Why not buttered rolls with different fillings?' suggested Adam.

'Far too much trouble,' said the dragon. 'I'm not spending my afternoon buttering buns and making fillings.'

'Someone else might,' said Adam.

'Who?' asked his brother.

'Well, you for a start.'

'No fear,' said John hastily.

The dragon waved his list. 'No need for all this talk,' he cried. 'It's veal and ham pies we're having. I thought we'd need a hundred.'

'It's cheaper to buy big ones and cut them into pieces,' said John.

'Ah, that's a good idea,' agreed the dragon. 'And we'll need several pots of mustard.' He scribbled on his list. 'I won't eat veal and ham pie without mustard. Then we'll have – but I'll read you the list.'

Sticking his pen behind one ear, he began:

'100 veal and ham pies. No, that's wrong.'

He took his pencil from behind his ear and made a correction.

'10 extra large veal and ham pies.
100 cheese and chutney sandwiches.'

'Who's going to cut them?' asked Adam.

'We'll buy them ready-made,' answered the dragon. 'Listen and don't interrupt. 100 assorted buns, doughnuts, chocolate éclairs, custard tarts, bakewell tarts, gingerbread, shortbread, Swiss buns, rock cakes, coconut kisses. I can't think of anything else. How's that?'

'Fabulous!' was Adam's reaction while John said approvingly: 'That ought to keep 'em from starvation,' but he added, 'I thought we'd decided against buns, because of buttering them.'

'Someone'll butter them,' said the dragon, 'and if they don't, we'll eat 'em *unbuttered*.'

Maurice and Jeff now appeared on the deck of *Money-Spider*. Denis, Hugh and Jean had been given a mooring in the cove on the opposite side of the harbour, and *Money-Spider* was back in her usual place alongside the dragon. The porthole had been mended. Jeff and Maurice seemed rather cross, and were in the middle of an argument. This upset Jacko. The dragon had taken his cover off, and the boys were scratching his head and talking to him while he was whistling happily in the early sunshine. But the sound of voices raised in argument always excited the parrot. He began to bob his head up and down. He bounced about on his perch and shrieked: 'Never say die! Never say die! No surrender! Have a banana! Oops-a-daisy!'

He then swung over and hung upside down, calling out in a sort of gabble: 'Good-old-Jacko! Polly-wolly-doodle!' Shrieks of raucous laughter followed these remarks, with repeated 'Oops-a-daisy'. At last he swung himself right way up and said loudly, in a rather conversational, gentlemanly tone: 'One, two, three, four – can say five but I won't!'

By this time Maurice and Jeff were on the quay. Maurice said angrily:

'O.K. You do what you like, Jeff. I'm going to the Club House to put through a call to Peter. It'll probably take some time to get through to Paris. It usually does, and of course he may not be in.'

'I don't see what he can do,' said Jeff gloomily.

'Well, at least I can tell him what's happened and he might have a few ideas about – well, *you* know – about –'

'Never say die!' shrieked Jacko suddenly.

'Oh, shut up!' shouted Maurice and started off down the quay towards the bridge.

'We're just going on a food-buying expedition,' said the dragon to Jeff, who was standing with his hands in his pockets, looking rather unhappy. 'Would you like to come with us?'

Jeff shrugged. 'Might as well,' he answered.

'You could help carry the things,' suggested Adam. 'Two hundred buns and all the doughnuts and whatever are going to take some carrying. Not to mention all those sandwiches.'

'And the veal and ham pies,' said John. 'We need to hire a trailer for *them*, I should think. The dragon could pull it.'

'What's all this in aid of?' asked Jeff.

So as they walked from the quay to St Mary's Street, the dragon explained about Fred and William being his old friends. He told the story of how he had wanted to get from Cornwall to St Aubyn's which was nearly three hundred miles away. Fred and William's removal van had been stuck in a narrow Cornish lane, and the dragon had heaved it off the bank and onto the road again. As the van was empty except for a piano, Fred and William offered to take the dragon in it up to St Aubyn's, near London, and, as they went, the dragon and William took it in turns to play the piano. They sang songs most of the way, with Fred driving. It had been a very jolly ride.

John was most impressed by the piano-playing, because he learned the piano himself. 'Can you really play the piano, Dragon?' he asked, rather disbelievingly.

'Oh, I can tickle the ivories if requested,' answered the dragon carelessly. 'One claw at a time, actually,' he added with a little cough.

At this moment they were just passing the Mary-Rose Café.

'Oh, look!' cried Adam. 'The notice about Sybil's gone, and there's a postcard!'

All four pressed their noses to the window of the Mary-Rose Café. Stuck against the glass with sellotape was a postcard, not the picture side but the side on which you write. It had a Jersey stamp and was addressed to: Mrs Prior, The Mary-Rose Café, Weymouth, England. John read it aloud:

'Don't worry about Sybil. We've got her aboard our yacht. She hid herself in the galley just before we left – wanted a holiday, we suppose. She's enjoyed sailing to Jersey very much. Back on Friday.'

'That's today!' cried the dragon. 'Let's go in and see if she's arrived yet.'

So they went into the café and there was Sybil as large as life, purring like a kettle on one of the chairs, very pleased with her trip to Jersey and back.

'Let's have coffee and a bun,' suggested the dragon.

But the boys were firm and steered him out onto the quay again, and in no time they had reached the shops.

'Now I think we ought to be fair,' said Adam, 'and get the food at lots of different places.'

The dragon and John and Jeff agreed. So they started off down St Mary's Street, and at the first likely shop they stopped and went in, leaving the dragon outside, staring at a window full of pies and sausages and the like. They came out bearing two large bags, containing the two biggest veal and ham pies that the shop sold. They set off down the street to find another butcher.

Almost at once the dragon stopped and said: 'I've had rather a good idea. An *important* idea.'

'What is it?' they all asked.

'I think I ought to sample everything to see if it's O.K.'

'Well, we've bought them now,' said Adam. 'If you

eat a bit of one of the pies, and say it's no good, I bet you the man won't take it back.'

'In that case, I won't do the pies, but I think I'll sample the other things – the doughnuts and coconut buns and so on.'

'Why shouldn't one of us do the sampling as well?' asked John.

'Or all of us?' added his brother.

'That would come far too expensive,' answered the dragon firmly.

'We could pay for the cake we sampled ourselves, couldn't we?' suggested Adam obstinately.

'You'd spoil your appetites for lunch,' said the dragon over his shoulder, as he pressed on up the street. 'That's what my old mother used to say.'

'What about you spoiling *your* appetite?' queried Adam, running to catch up with the dragon.

'I shall count the sampling as my lunch,' retorted the dragon and puffed out some green smoke, for he was feeling full of bright ideas. 'And I may add that it'll probably be the first decent meal I've had since I came to Weymouth.'

'I refuse to go on,' said John, 'unless we all share in the sampling, or give up the idea.'

The dragon stopped dead. He felt there was mutiny in the ranks. He thought furiously what answer he could make to this when Jeff poured oil on the troubled waters.

'Oh, come on, all of you!' he said. 'Let's get some more things bought before we decide about the sampling. We're just wasting time.'

It was the buns and cakes next. The dragon wouldn't let anyone go into the shop until he had pointed with a claw at each kind of cake he wanted. Then John went in and bought a mixed bag, and the dragon insisted that they should all walk up to the esplanade, sit near the sea and eat something from the bag there. 'It'll be like a picnic,' he said. 'Brunch for you, lunch for me, a cake for each of you and – er – two cakes for me.'

'It'll be like several picnics,' said Jeff, 'if we do this with every shop.'

'Well, why not?' asked the dragon with a genial grin. 'It seems to me a thoroughly good idea.'

By the time they had sampled the cakes of the fourth shop, everyone was getting rather tired and cross, not least the dragon.

'I think I'll take a snooze,' he said in grumbling tones, 'and we can start again this afternoon.'

The others looked at each other. Then Jeff spoke out: 'That's not an awfully good idea, Dragon. I think we ought to get the job finished. It's nearly half-past twelve and most of the shops close for lunch. I vote we go back the way we came and just buy more of each kind, till we've got the right number.'

'I thought I was –' began the dragon, but Jeff cut in quickly: 'We'll take a show of hands. Those in favour of my idea?'

Adam and John put up their hands.

'Anyone against?'

'Oh, all right,' agreed the dragon. 'Come on.'

It was well after one o'clock when they reached the quay. They put the food in the kitchen of the Jolly Sailor, and then the dragon looked round at his helpers.

'Actually,' he said, 'I will confess that my idea was not all that good. It proved to be very tiring. Also, I'm extremely full. I don't know about all of you.'

'I don't think we ate quite so much,' said John, 'but I'm thirsty.'

'So am I,' said the dragon, 'and I'm going to reward you for all your noble help this morning. Into the bar with you, and here's my purse. Buy yourselves a drink apiece and bring me out a pint of that special beer.'

Adam was too young to be allowed in a bar. So was John really, but he was tall, and looked older than he was, so he went in with Jeff, holding the dragon's seaweed purse in his hand. When he had paid for the drinks, he said to Jeff: 'I say, this party's cost the dragon an awful lot. There's hardly any money left in his purse.'

'Tell you what,' said Jeff. 'We'll have a quiet whip-round at the party tonight. Just among his friends. Then we can pay him back.'

'Good idea,' said John. 'I'm going to dash back home and tell mother we're not in for lunch, we've eaten too much.'

Jeff sat down on the edge of the quay after fetching a second pint of beer, and lit a cigarette. Adam joined the Leaners, who were gazing silently at the harbour as they ate sandwiches and drank beer.

'Did you hear about the police going to the Spider's Web?' asked Adam.

'Aye,' said Bill. 'We heard.'

'It was awfully interesting, seeing how they got the door open. Like burglars.'

'Ah, that would ha' been interesting,' agreed George.

'D'you know Mr Spicer?' went on Adam.

'Suppose I do,' answered Bill vaguely.

'We do, too, John and me,' said Adam.

'Do you, then? What do you know?' asked Bill.

'Well, we bought a telescope from him last year and the glass fell out, and he wouldn't give us our money back.'

'Wouldn't he? No, I don't suppose he would.'

'D'you like Mr Spicer?' asked Adam, determined to find out something more.

'Can't say I like him or don't like him,' said George. 'Never thought about it.'

'My brother John says he's a fence.'

At this, the Leaners took their pipes out of their mouths and stared at Adam.

'Does he now?' said George.

'Ain't that a bit of guesswork?' suggested Bill.

'Well, yes,' admitted Adam, 'but it's interesting all the same.'

'Other people's affairs is always interesting,' said George, 'but you want to be careful what you say about 'em.'

Both men replaced their pipes and looked so fixedly across the harbour that Adam felt it was useless to question them any more. He could see John coming back from the boarding-house, and he didn't feel that John would be altogether pleased at him questioning the Leaners.

The dragon had lowered himself into the water and was preparing himself for his usual afternoon nap when he heard a familiar voice. The Secretary of the Yacht Club was passing by.

'Aha!' he said. 'The old sea-serpent's still here, I see!'

The dragon opened his eyes and said very quickly: 'I am not –'

'No, no, I quite understand. I'm not sure that I do think you're a sea-serpent now. They're usually brown. Mud-coloured. You're a fabulous beast, aren't you? In fact, I don't know that I believe in you at all. I may be just seeing things.'

'You're seeing me,' said the dragon, 'and I am a –'

'Not a bit of it, my dear chap. Don't try to explain. I'm seeing things. That's what it is. I've always had this gift. Saw a melusine once – you ever met a melusine?'

'Well, actually –' began the dragon.

'No, very unlikely. They're rare. Mermaid with two tails, you know. Two tails. Very charming. I saw one once. Or did I? You see, it may be just my gift for seeing things that no one else can see. I hooked a small sea-serpent once. No one would believe me.'

'But I am not –' but the dragon had no chance.

'Yes, hooked it and pulled it aboard. But it slipped off the hook back into the sea. Never saw it again. Good day to you all! I must be getting on my way.' And the Secretary disappeared in the direction of the Town Bridge.

The dragon heaved an immense sigh and closed his eyes. Soon after this, Fred and William emerged from the Jolly Sailor as it was about to shut, and walked over towards the dragon.

'He's asleep, I think,' said Jeff, who was still sitting on the edge of the quay with an empty beer tankard beside him.

'Oh, well, we'll see him later, of course. At the party,' said Fred, and he and William began to walk away, when Jeff got to his feet quickly and said:

'I wonder if I could ask you something.'

'Ask away,' said Fred.

'You run a removals business, don't you?'

'We do. Three vans we've got now,' said William.

'Well, my mate and I have got some – er – a small quantity of stuff on the – that is, in Weymouth, that we want taken up to London. Any chance of you being able to do the job?'

'Depends how much there is,' said William.

'Well, not a great deal. Nothing large. A few card-board boxes.'

'What is it, then? Bits of junk?'

'Yes, that's right,' said Jeff. 'We were going to sell it at the Spider's Web, but he seems to be away, so we thought we'd be better off selling it in London.'

'Where is it now?'

Before he could stop himself, Jeff said, without thinking: 'It's on the boat, of course.'

'On the boat?' Jeff could have bitten his tongue. 'Where d'you buy it then?' asked Fred.

'In Boulogne,' said Jeff hastily. 'There's a lot of junk-shops there.'

'It seems a funny sort of business to me,' said Fred, unbelievingly. 'But it's your affair, of course. We don't want to get mixed up with anything – anything illegal, you know. And there's other junk-shops in Weymouth as well as the Spider's Web, if you want to sell it now.'

'Of course there are,' said Jeff. 'But actually some of it's quite valuable, Maurice thinks, and we might get a better price for it in London.'

'O.K. We'll do it,' said Fred.

'When could you take it?'

'Not for three days,' said William firmly. 'It's nearly the weekend to start with. And we haven't got a van available. We've got one half full, and waiting for a consignment of furniture – then she'll go off to the north. Our other two vans are both away. Due back in two or three days.'

'And on top of that,' said Fred, 'we're losing our small warehouse at the end of this week. Council won't rent it to us no longer, 'cos they want to pull it down. We got to find another place. In fact, we're going to look at a place this afternoon. Let us know if you want us to take your stuff next week.'

And with that, Fred and William went off. John and Adam had gone to Osmington by bus to have a swim.

Jeff was left kicking his heels on the quay, but he didn't have to wait long before Maurice came in sight.

'You've been ages,' said Jeff.

'O.K. I've been ages. But I've been doing something practical, not just loafing on the quay,' said Maurice.

'What about brother Peter?'

'I got him in the end, and he said I'd best get a self-drive car and take the stuff up to his place in London. So I found a garage which does self-drive, and I've booked a car. Couldn't get one till Tuesday which is a curse, but can't be helped.'

Jeff said nothing. Maurice turned sharply on him.

'What's the matter? Why don't you say something?' he demanded.

'I'm sorry,' answered Jeff, 'but as a matter of fact, I've made an arrangement as well.'

'An arrangement? What arrangement?'

'Well, there's been a couple of removals men here, that I've got to know. They have a small business of their

own, with three vans, and they've got a van going to London next week, so I asked them to take the stuff.'

'You clot!' shouted Maurice. 'I suppose you told them what it was, too?'

'I didn't. I said it was bits of junk we'd picked up in Boulogne.'

'Well, you'll have to cancel your arrangement with them,' said Maurice. 'The fewer people concerned in this the better. I'll drive the stuff up myself on Tuesday. You can stay behind and look after the boat.'

'O.K.,' said Jeff. 'I suppose I'd better try and find these men now and cancel the arrangement.'

'You do that,' said Maurice. 'I can't think why you're such a clot!'

The parrot suddenly uttered a squawk, and then shrieked: 'Clot! Clot! Here we go again!'

Maurice picked up the baize cloth cover and dropped it over the cage.

'The next thing,' he said, 'we'll be having that parrot broadcasting our affairs all over the harbour. I'm going aboard to have a sleep.'

He walked across the dragon, who was fast asleep, and disappeared into *Money-Spider*'s cabin.

9

A Letter Leads up to the Party

LATER that afternoon, John and Adam came along the quay after their swim at Osmington Mills, and found the dragon in a state of great excitement.

'D'you know what?' he exclaimed as soon as he saw them. 'A few minutes ago, the postman brought me a letter from my Aunt Dracula. Second post.'

'Aunt Dracula? The one who lives at Longleat?' asked John, rubbing his still damp red hair with an even damper towel.

'That's the one. Anyway there could only be one Aunt Dracula.'

'We've been to Longleat,' said Adam. 'Twice. I don't remember seeing a dragon there.'

The dragon looked at Adam with pained surprise. 'My dear Adam,' he said. 'My Aunt Dracula is not on display in the park, like those common animals, the lions and warthogs and their kind. She lives with the family at Longleat House. The Marquess has given her very comfortable quarters in the West Wing. On the ground floor. She finds stairs rather trying now. She's not as young as she was.'

'Doesn't she ever go out?' asked Adam, who was feeling cold and miserable, as he usually did after a swim, and wanted badly to get back to the boarding-house.

'Of course she goes out. She is out most of the day, round and about the park, observing the antics of the human beings. When I read you her letter you'll see why you didn't see her. She's usually invisible even when she's there.'

'Could I go and get a drink from the café first?' asked Adam, his teeth chattering.

'Oh, for heaven's sake, Adam!' expostulated his brother. 'Go and get your drink. I want to hear Aunt Dracula's letter, so buck up.'

While Adam shambled over to the café, John tickled Jacko with a straw he'd picked up, and the dragon asked him if the swimming was good at Osmington.

'It's not bad,' answered John. 'But I think you might like it there for a different reason.'

'Oh, indeed! What?' asked the dragon.

'There's a pub there does lobster teas. We didn't have one today, of course, and they're awfully expensive but jolly well worth it if you're having a birthday or something like that.'

'I must remember that pub,' said the dragon. 'I'm very partial to a lobster tea.'

Adam then reappeared, carrying a plastic mug of coffee and two bags.

'I thought we all needed fortifying if we're going to listen to a long letter,' he said. 'Here, Dragon, I bought you a crab sandwich –'

'Adam!' cried the dragon. 'You are a prince among boys!'

'And I got you one, too,' Adam went on, handing another fat sandwich to his brother.

'Good for you!' exclaimed John.

'Shall I begin reading?' asked the dragon, whose sandwich had disappeared as if by magic.

'O.K.' and 'Please do!' cried the two boys through their mouthfuls.

The dragon unfolded the letter and began.

West Wing,
Longleat House,
Wiltshire
July 20th

My dear nephew,

I trust you are well. I was delighted to get your postcard. What a pretty harbour! Weymouth must be a charming place except for the trippers. Of course, you're not really used to them, as I am –

The dragon looked up and put in: 'She should just see what we get in Cornwall!' Then he went on:

Here at Longleat I am never free of them because I have to listen to them and watch them continually day in and day out, to get material for my Great Work. I don't know if I told you the title I have chosen for it. It is this: *Humans on Safari: A Study of Human Behaviour.*

I recently designed a useful 'hide' – the kind of thing humans use for watching birds, poor deluded creatures, as if they could understand a thing about the commonest sparrow. But let that pass. The head gardener built the 'hide' for me, a long tunnel-like structure in which I can recline comfortably. It is made of bamboo canes covered with imitation grass and leaves. Very effective and light, so that it can be moved about easily.

I could fill pages for you, drawn from my observations on human beings, but I will only mention the behaviour of their cubs. No discipline. No manners. Personally, were I a mother, I should be *most* relieved to see my offspring eaten by a lion. They would be no loss. But humans seem to *dote* upon their cubs, and actually *reward* their noisy and often unruly and destructive behaviour with a seemingly endless supply of ice-creams, lollies and bubble-gum. I have found several pieces of the latter stuck to my 'hide'. No matter. One must expect to suffer for one's art and the book is making good progress.

Let me hear from you again, dear nephew. Any details about the particular species of human being in your area will be very welcome.

Your affectionate
Aunt Dracula

The boys were sitting with their legs dangling over the water, and had finished their sandwiches.

'This coffee's awful,' remarked Adam.

'Adam,' said the dragon severely. 'Have you really been listening to my Aunt Dracula's letter?'

'Of course I have!' protested Adam. 'I was just going to ask you, will you really send her notes about people who come along the quay?'

'Certainly. I shall buy a notebook, I think, specially for writing down what I observe. I might be very helpful to my aunt. She might even mention me in the Preface to her book.'

'Would you like that?' asked John.

'Of course, and so would you,' retorted the dragon. 'And don't pretend that you wouldn't. I dedicated my Memoirs to a little girl called Susan, and she never got over it. Has the page framed over her mantelpiece, I believe.'

'I think that's silly,' said Adam.

The dragon looked at him in silence for a moment. Then he said: 'If you think that's silly, Adam, it merely shows that you have the wrong ideas.'

'Not wrong. Different,' said John, who liked an argument.

'Wrong,' repeated the dragon firmly and sent out an angry puff of green smoke towards the boys, which unfortunately was blown off course by the wind and landed on the top of the parrot cage, waking Jacko, who had been dozing up till then.

'All aboard!' he shrieked. 'All aboard!' and then gave a shrill whistle. This attracted the attention of some passers-by, who walked over to the edge of the quay, where the parrot-cage stood, and found themselves looking down upon a large green dragon, with yellow tips to his horns. One party consisted of a mother and father and a rather fat, pimply boy. They stood in a row immediately above the dragon's head. When he looked up and said politely: 'Good afternoon! Wonderful weather, isn't it?' the boy exclaimed:

'Coo! He's got no teef!'

The dragon scowled. He shut his jaws with a snap and muttered through his toothless gums: 'Oh, yes, I have!'

'Can't see 'em, then.'

'My teeth are invisible,' hissed the dragon, and the boy backed hastily away. *His* teeth, the dragon observed, stuck out in a most unattractive way. 'Ought to wear a brace,' thought the dragon, making a mental note that he would mention this feature when he next wrote to Aunt Dracula.

'Come along, Cyril,' said his mother.

'I wanna see his invisible teef!' whined Cyril.

'Don't be so daft!' exclaimed his dad. 'How can you see 'em if they're invisible?'

'I wanna see 'em!' bawled Cyril.

'You stop that!' said his mother, giving him a shake. 'Another word and you don't get an ice-cream.'

This silenced Cyril at once. His eyes shone and, giving an enormous sniff, he cried: 'There's a shop with ice-cream!' and pointed up the quay. Soon he was licking his way round a large cornet, the kind with a stick of flaky chocolate stuck into the top of it. He rushed back to the dragon, waving his cornet and jeered: 'Yah! Don't care about your silly teef, see!'

The dragon turned his head towards him very quickly and breathed out a small but fierce blast of green smoke towards the ice-cream cornet which promptly started to melt. As Cyril waved it wildly about, trying to control the runny ice-cream, first the chocolate flake and then the whole cornet fell into the harbour.

Cyril's dad strode up the quay. 'I saw you!' he shouted at the dragon. 'I'll report you to the police for that!

Taking our Cyril's ice-cream. What you done with it? Eh? What you done with it?'

'He's eaten it!' screamed Cyril. 'He's eaten it all up!'

The dragon beckoned to Adam with a yellow claw, and when Adam bent towards him, the dragon whispered: 'I've melted his ice, the little beast, and I can't stand his howling – it's enough to make me throw *him* into the harbour. And now Dad's joined in – listen to him carrying on! I'd like to toss him in too. For heaven's sake, Adam, buy the child another cornet and get him away from here before I go mad. I'll pay you back.'

Adam ran at top speed to the shop and bought Cyril an even larger cornet with *two* flaky chocolate bars stuck into the ice-cream, and presented this to the snivelling Cyril, who didn't even say thank you. His irate parents, still muttering threats of the police, grabbed their little horror and dragged him from the scene. The dragon took his purse from his left ear and handed Adam a pound note.

'I haven't the change for that,' said Adam.

'Never mind!' cried the dragon recklessly. 'It was worth a pound to get rid of Cyril. If ever you see him without his mum and dad, just oblige me by pushing him into the harbour. I must make a rule: never speak to trippers.'

'Not all trippers are nasty,' said John, who had quietly observed the scene from further along the quay. He was eating crisps which he'd just bought. 'Have a crisp, Dragon?'

'Thanks, I will. You couldn't get another packet, could you? My nerves are frazzled. They need food to calm them down.'

'O.K., you have this bag,' said John, handing it to the dragon.

'But it's half-eaten,' he complained.

'I'll get another packet,' laughed John.

'About trippers,' he said, as he walked back with his crisps. 'We're trippers, really, aren't we? Adam and me. And so are you, old dragon. You've come here on a trip, a dragon's trip.'

'A dragon's trip is quite different from anyone else's,' said the dragon, delicately wiping pieces of crisp from his mouth with a handkerchief with D in the corner (it had been made for him by the mermaid).

'Why?' demanded Adam.

This flummoxed the dragon, who could only think of saying: 'Because I'm R. Dragon.'

'Well, I'm Adam and he's John,' argued the boy. 'We're different from everyone else, too, but we're still trippers.'

'There are probably several categories of tripper,' remarked John, thoughtfully.

'Cater-what?' asked the dragon.

'It means several kinds,' explained John. 'Adam trippers and John trippers and Cyril trippers, and of course dragon trippers.'

'This conversation is getting boring,' said the dragon and yawned.

'And we'd better be getting back and see what's on for the afternoon,' said John.

'It's the party tonight. What time does it start?' asked Adam.

The dragon suggested that it should start about eight,

and said he'd be glad if the boys could write one or two notices and put them up at the Jolly Sailor and in one or two of the quay shops.

'We'll do that,' said Adam, and then turning to his brother said: 'Why don't we have a look at that scruffy old building behind the boarding-house? Mrs Simmonds owns it. She might give us the key and we could ask her if she wants to let it.'

'You mean for William and Fred?' queried John. When Adam nodded, he went on: 'She told me it was an old sail-loft. I don't think she uses it for anything. Good idea of yours, Adam.'

The boys went off, the dragon dozed, Jacko made quiet gabbling noises and whistled tunefully, and so the hot afternoon passed peacefully by, with hardly anything going on in the harbour or on the deserted quays.

It was much later that the dragon woke up with a start. 'Something special's happening,' he muttered to himself. 'Where's everybody got to? And *whatever* was it we were – OF COURSE!' he almost bellowed. 'It's our PARTY!' And just then he heard the clock on St Mary's church tower strike the hour of six. He untied his mooring rope and climbed onto the quay. Here he opened his suitcase.

'I wonder if I'll need my teeth,' he thought. 'Possibly I shall. Yes, I'll put them in.' He opened a long wooden box, rather like a pencil-box, and removed a set of white, pointed teeth. Looking carefully around him to make sure that no one saw him, he popped them into his mouth. They clicked into place, and the dragon leant over the edge of the quay, gave a beaming smile and saw his reflection in the water – the wide grin and the splendid set of teeth. 'Fine!' he said to himself, and then turned his expression into a snarl. 'Gosh! That's enough to frighten anyone!' he muttered. He then took a comb out of his suitcase and tidied the few hairs that grew between his ears.

'My claws,' he said to himself, inspecting them. 'Disgraceful! Must clean them.'

He searched again in his suitcase and found a little piece of fishbone which he always used as a claw-cleaner. Each of his twenty yellow claws was scrupulously cleaned and then rubbed on a corner of the baize cage-cover to polish them.

Jacko watched these operations with one black, beady eye, while the other eye was observing the passers-by and anything else that interested his parrot mind. He kept up an almost continuous whistling, for he felt very happy, sitting in the sunshine, being admired by almost every man, woman and child who came by.

At last the dragon was satisfied with his appearance and said: 'Well, Jacko, what shall we do next?'

'Oops-a-daisy!' muttered Jacko in a low voice.

'Food,' said the dragon thoughtfully. 'Yes, I'd better see what's happening about the food.'

He walked over to the Jolly Sailor and put his head in at the bar.

'Good evening all!' he said politely.

A general cry of 'Good evening!' and similar greetings made him feel very welcome and he smiled with pleasure upon the company in the bar, and accepted with an almost courtly bow a tankard of the Jolly Sailor's best. A honking and tooting outside on the quay made him back out of the bar carefully. He realized that his backlegs and long tail were lying right across the road and a couple of cars were unable to get by.

'Sorry!' called the dragon. 'My apologies!'

He moved his long body and placed himself along the pavement. When he had finished his tankard of beer, he handed it through the door of the bar and asked where the kitchen was.

'You needn't worry about the food for the party tonight,' said the barman, who was also the owner of the pub. 'The wife's in there and she's got our girl Laura helping her, not to mention Daisy.'

129

'Daisy?' repeated the dragon. 'Would that be my friend George Snook's Daisy?'

'That's her,' said the barman.

'You can always trust old Daisy to turn up if there's a fête or a flower show,' said one of the company. 'Very good at buttering rolls is our George Snook's Daisy.'

So the dragon took himself round to the back of the pub and looked in at the kitchen door. There were the barman's wife and daughter, Laura, working away. Both were wearing aprons of gaily printed cotton and the wife, whose name was Lil, had her hair done up in curlers.

'You'll excuse my hair, won't you, dear?' she said to the dragon. 'It's that steamy in here, it takes all the curl out of yer hair.'

'Think nothing of it, Mrs – er – Mrs –' faltered the dragon, realizing too late that he didn't know the surname of the barman.

'Lil's the name,' said the barman's wife, laughing in a jolly manner that the dragon liked very much. 'And me husband is Bertram and this young lady here is me daughter Laura.'

The dragon beamed on them both and then turned his attention to the third lady, a white-haired, thin and bony woman. She wore a tightly-wrapped overall which must have belonged to George, for it was much too big for her. It reached to her ankles and was wound round her and kept in place by a tightly-knotted piece of string.

The dragon said good evening to her, and asked if he might call her Daisy.

'It's as you like, dear,' she said.

The dragon had never before been addressed as 'dear' by anyone, and rather liked it. It was warm and homely.

He thanked the three ladies very much for all the work they were doing.

'We couldn't run a party without the ladies, could we?' he observed. 'It was just the same in King Arthur's day.' He leant against the door and folded his forelegs across his chest. 'If there was a feast, the ladies moved into the kitchen for at least a week beforehand, to supervise the cooking of the boars' heads, and the marinating of the venison in wine, the stirring of the hubble-bubble, and the making of the famous Tintagel tarts.' A faraway look appeared in the dragon's eyes. 'Ah, those Tintagel tarts!' he murmured. 'I'll never taste their like again.'

'Haven't you got the recipe for 'em?' asked Lil the barman's wife.

'Alas, no,' sighed the dragon. 'It was never written down. It was just passed on from one cook to another.'

'Well, then,' said Mrs Daisy Snook briskly. 'You'll just have to be content with buttered buns, won't you, instead of yer tintack tarts or whatever they're called.'

'And what's nicer than a buttered bun?' cried the dragon. 'Mrs Snook, I've never seen a bun buttered as well as you're doing it.'

'Eh?' said George Snook's lady.

'You are the best butterer I ever saw, a queen among butter-ladies,' said the dragon, and with this compliment, he reached out a paw and caught Daisy's buttery hand in his green paw and kissed it.

'Oh, lawks!' exclaimed Daisy, going very pink. 'What a lovely gentleman, or I suppose I should say – dragon –'

The dragon couldn't reach the hands of the other two ladies to kiss them, so he blew them each a green smoke kiss and backed out into the street. As he emerged onto the quay, he saw Fred and William coming along towards him. In no time, the three of them had planned the final details of the party.

'We'll get the piano out on the quay,' said Fred.

'Righty-ho!' agreed William. 'What about tables for the food?'

'We need trestle tables,' said the dragon, scratching his head.

'Leave it to us,' said Fred.

'Did I hear you say trestle tables?' called out Bill Pouncy who was just going into the Jolly Sailor for his early evening pint. 'The people who run the Mary-Rose Café along the quay have got some tables they use at Carnival time. Keep 'em in a shed at the back, a' believe.'

So Fred and William went off to try and borrow them, and the dragon strolled up and down the quay in front of the Jolly Sailor, feeling very happy at the thought of the party. As he strolled, he remembered the time when he had travelled up to St Aubyn's, near London, in the back of Fred and William's removal van, that had painted on the outside these words:

WE TAKE
ANYTHING
ANYWHERE
ANY TIME.

He remembered, too, the piano in the back of the van and the song he sang, just as they were packing up his belongings to leave Cornwall for the journey.

'One of my best songs ever,' mused the dragon, and, as he paced up and down on the quay, he sang it quietly under his breath.

It went to the tune of *Old MacDonald had a Farm*.

> '*Old R. Dragon had a ride*
> *In Fred and William's van-o!*
> *And on that ride he sang some songs,*
> *In Fred and William's van-o!*
> *With a toot-toot here,*
> *And a honk-honk there,*
> *Here a toot, there a toot,*
> *Here and there a honk-honk!*'

'Ah, me! Happy days!' said the dragon to himself. 'But tonight we'll be together again, and it's going to be a splendid party!'

10

The Garland of Friendship

ABOUT seven o'clock that evening, Fred and William appeared on the quay.

'We thought we'd jolly things up a bit,' they explained, as they unrolled some long strings of bunting, and set down several cardboard boxes.

'What's in the boxes?' asked the dragon at once. 'Not – it couldn't be – some sort of *food*, could it? I wouldn't mind a snack. It seems a long time since I had a square meal. In fact, I haven't had a *square* meal today. Only a rather small round one. Or, to be truthful, several very small round ones.'

'Sorry, Dragon,' said Fred. 'There's no food in them boxes. Only fairy lights. Reckon you might find them a bit indigestible.'

'Then while you're putting them up, perhaps I'd better go back to the kitchen and help them with the food,' suggested the dragon.

'How do you mean – help them?' asked Fred, giving the dragon a stern look with just the hint of a smile.

'Oh, you know – put buns out onto plates, decorate the sandwiches with parsley – that sort of thing,' said the dragon carelessly, buffing his claws on his chest.

William's long, serious face turned towards the dragon. 'If you're really hungry, that might be a good idea,' he said. 'Only, Dragon, don't you get those claws of yours on too many of these here comestibles, or there mightn't be any left for the party.'

'Comestibles?' exclaimed the dragon. 'If that's another word for food, I don't care for it. It's too like indigestible.'

'Well, whatever it is, don't eat too much of it,' Fred called out, but the dragon was already out of sight, padding quickly up the side street to the kitchen door of the Jolly Sailor. He put his head in and called out: 'How's the comestibles? That means food.'

There was no one there to his great disappointment. The table and the white work-tops round two sides of the room were covered with tablecloths, looking oddly bumpy and uneven. The dragon cautiously lifted the corner of one with his claw.

'Aha!' he said under his breath. 'Here we are!' For under the white cloths lay plates of sandwiches and doughnuts and éclairs and buttered buns and all the other goodies that he had bought and the womenfolk had prepared that afternoon. The dragon's mouth watered. He reached out his other paw, and let it hover over a doughnut – then over a bun – it twitched slightly, and moved back to the doughnut.

'Come on, then, Laura. Help us get the food onto the trestle tables. It's nearly half-past seven.' The voice was Daisy Snook's. There was a sound of feet in the passage. The dragon dropped the cloth guiltily and blushed a little. His yellow horns went quite pink. The kitchen door then opened and in came Lil, Daisy and Laura.

'Hullo, Dragon!' they all exclaimed, much surprised to see him.

'Aha!' he replied, not very convincingly, and added: 'Oho!'

'Oho what?' asked Daisy.

'I'm here,' said the dragon.

'So we see,' said Lil.

'I've come to help,' said the dragon.

'Well, that's nice,' said Lil.

'There seems to be a lot of stuff to carry out,' went on the dragon, now feeling better and kidding himself that of course he would *never* have taken that doughnut.

The women whisked the cloths off the food and took them out to spread over the trestle tables. Then they started to carry out the plates of food, but almost at once Lil said: 'I don't know about you, Daisy, but we've worked hard and I'm fair peckish. I don't see why we shouldn't have a sandwich or something to keep us going.'

She picked out a sandwich and took a bite. Daisy chose a gingerbread slice and Laura a doughnut.

The dragon looked at them sorrowfully, especially at Laura. *He* hadn't been working all the afternoon. He'd just been snoozing. So he didn't like to take anything, but he gave a little cough and said in a very low voice, almost a whisper: 'Laura, is that doughnut nice?'

'Super,' replied Laura, her mouth all sugary.

'How's your sandwich, Mrs – er –?' he asked.

'Very tasty,' she replied. 'Do call me Lil.'

'And the gingerbread, Daisy?' The dragon's voice now sounded quite faint.

'Not bad,' answered Daisy. 'Not as nice as what I make

136

meself. But – my sakes alive! Why aren't *you* having anything, Dragon?'

'I'm not really hungry,' muttered the dragon, earnestly inspecting his right paw.

'Oh, come on!' cried Daisy.

'Don't make him, if he doesn't want anything yet,' said Laura.

But the dragon had already taken a doughnut. The women then started to carry out the food, and he licked the sugar off his claws and very quickly ate a sandwich when no one was looking.

'Lovely doughnuts, aren't they?' remarked the dragon to anyone who had time to listen. Actually his mouth was full of sandwich.

'That's nice,' said Daisy. 'Now you can help us take out the last few plates and then we're ready. And oh my, Dragon! Just wait till you see what's been done outside! It looks like Christmas Day and Carnival Week rolled into one!'

And it really did. The dragon gave a gasp when he saw it and almost dropped the plate of buttered buns. Fred and William had hung long streamers of brightly-coloured bunting from the pub to telegraph poles, and along the quay from one lamp-post to the next. They had put fairy lights round the Jolly Sailor's windows, and also round the top of the parrot-cage, inside which Jacko was whistling cheerfully and calling out remarks like 'All aboard!' and 'Whoops-a-daisy!'

'Looks kind of festive, doesn't it?' said the usually gloomy William, a smile widening across his lantern jaws.

'It looks absolutely beautiful!' cried the dragon. 'It's

going to be the loveliest party. When are we going to start?'

'Well,' said William, 'there's just one thing more to do, and that is to get the piano out of the pub. Fred's just gone in to ask for help with it. Ah, here he comes.'

The pub door opened and Fred came out backwards, at one end of the piano, while three or four other stalwarts heaved it over the pavement and onto the roadway.

'Where's she to go?' asked one.

'Over here,' cried the dragon. 'Where I'm standing.'

So they heaved it over and William opened the lid, and the dragon played two or three notes with one claw and felt extremely excited.

'What shall we sing to start the party off?' he asked Fred and William.

'What about starting with *It's a long way to Tipperary*?' suggested Fred. 'Everyone knows that.'

'I've never understood where Tipperary was,' remarked the dragon. 'I know I've never been there.'

'It's in Ireland,' said William.

'Why do we have to go there?' asked the dragon. 'I mean, what's the point?'

'We don't and there isn't any,' said John, who had just arrived. 'Silly old dragon – it's only a way of saying that it's a long way to wherever you're going.'

'Well, it was a long way here from Cornwall,' said the dragon. 'So I vote we start with that song, and we'll alter the words a bit.'

So Fred and William and the dragon all got into a huddle to work out some new words to the old song, *Tipperary*, but they found it very difficult to make any new words fit the tune.

'Here are the boys,' cried the dragon, seeing John and Adam walking towards them. 'Perhaps they can help us think.'

John went into the Jolly Sailor and Adam asked: 'Help you do what?'

'Make up some new words to *Tipperary*.'

'I don't know the old words,' said Adam. 'Anyway, it's food and drink people are coming for, not a singsong.'

The dragon looked rather put out and was trying to think of something crushing to say to Adam, when the boy pulled some pieces of paper out of his pocket and said: 'I've got some new jokes and riddles for the party.'

'They'll have to come later,' said the dragon quickly, hoping that this would show Adam what he thought of him, but Adam merely grinned and said: 'O.K., O.K. Why's William sitting at the piano?'

'We've got to get everyone together, so he's going to play *Tipperary* and we're all going to sing like mad. You included, Adam, words or not, and you too, John.' John was just coming out of the pub, looking very grown-up with a glass of beer in one hand, and a bottle of coke in the other, which he gave to Adam.

'I can't sing,' said John promptly.

'Never mind – shout!' commanded the dragon. 'That's right, William, give us a chord. That's too high. Put it lower. Now – one, two, three – *It's a –*'

Off they went, dragon, Fred, William, and a few by-standers. Their voices echoed from the warehouse walls and caused quite a stir among the yachts and dinghies, now sailing quietly into the harbour in the evening light. Jacko was inspired to lift up his voice also, so the general effect was like this:

It's a long way to Tipperary –

Oops-a-daisy!

It's a long way to go!

Never say die!

It's a long way –

Here we go again!

The fairy lights and the singing soon began to attract people. The landlord, Ben Jackson, wearing a white apron and a black bowler hat, presided over barrels of beer and cider inside the actual bar, with the doors wide open, and Mrs Jackson, that is Lil, had put on a flowered silk dress and taken the curlers out of her hair. It now clustered in bright golden curls all over her head. She handed round plates and urged people to eat. Everyone wanted to know why the party was being held, so the dragon had a wonderful time telling the same story over and over again – how he first met Fred and William in Cornwall, and now after all these years (he wasn't sure how many because dragons only think in hundreds) here they were all together again on Weymouth quay.

The dragon's manners impressed one and all. 'Quite the gentleman, isn't he?' whispered one lady to her husband.

At last, when everyone was well away with the eats and drinks, the dragon announced that there would be a singsong in about half-an-hour, when they had all had enough to eat and drink.

'Can you all eat and drink enough in half-an-hour?' he asked anxiously, but the murmurs of 'That's O.K.!' and 'Course we can!' died away into silence as all eyes turned towards a small creature who had jumped onto the piano stool and then onto the piano top, and was sitting there, surveying the whole company.

'Sybil!' came numerous exclamations, and 'Sybil's back, hooray!' For it was indeed the cat of the Mary-Rose Café, the cat with mackerel-like tabby markings, who had been on an unexpected joy-ride to Jersey and back.

For a moment the dragon felt worried. It was not, after all, Sybil's party, yet here she was, right in the limelight. Then he quelled such ignoble thoughts, and advanced towards her.

'Delighted you are back, Sybil,' he said, stretching out his huge paw to take one of her elegant small ones.

'*Noblesse oblige!*' he cried, using the only French phrase he knew, and kissed Sybil's paw.

There was cheering and a burst of applause. Sybil purred, and having climbed down from the piano she stalked about among the guests, welcoming them all in a most gracious manner, and the dragon didn't mind too much, because she did it so charmingly. When he thought the eating and drinking was nearly over, he announced that there would now be the singsong, and people gathered round the piano. The piano-movers had carefully avoided putting the piano across the road, in the way of passing cars. They had pulled it towards the edge of the quay, but they had not noticed that it was now fair and square across the railway track, along which ran the trains that carried passengers and luggage to the Channel Islands ferry-boats. Even if anyone *had* noticed, they might have thought it hardly mattered, since the next train didn't come along until after eleven o'clock that evening.

It was now nearly nine. The harbour lights were twinkling in the dusk, casting their bright reflections onto the water, reflections that broke into a thousand gold pieces every time a yacht or launch disturbed the surface. You could see the light winking in the little lighthouse on the end of the stone pier, as the bay and the distant cliffs darkened to a deep blue and the pinpoints of light on the sea far beyond the harbour marked the boats of night-fishermen.

William and Fred and the dragon soon had everyone singing, and there were several people eager to play the piano, which by this time had a row of beer-mugs along its top. Jeff was among the crowd round the piano, and so were the Leaners. The Harbour-Master passed by and was persuaded to have a drink with the dragon in the lull between two songs. They clinked their glasses solemnly and the dragon cried:

'A toast! Listen, everyone!' Then he whispered something in the Harbour-Master's ear.

'The dragon has asked me to propose the loyal toast,' he said. 'Ladies and gentlemen, cats, dragons and parrots – the Queen – God bless her!'

Everyone clinked glasses but before they could burst into song again or talk, the dragon held up his glass and bellowed in his most dragonish voice:

'Here's my toast, and William's and Fred's and all of us friends on the quay: MAY THE GARLAND OF FRIENDSHIP EVER BE GREEN!'

There was a clinking of glasses, and Daisy wiped her eyes and said it was the most beautiful toast she had ever heard, and, almost at once, people started singing:

142

'For he's a jolly good dragon!
For he's a jolly good dragon!
For he's a jolly good dragon!
And so say all of us!'

The dragon was now as moved as Daisy and had to brush away a tear or two quickly with his scaly paw.

People started dancing on the quay, while William played a rousing tune. Suddenly a new sound was heard above the piano and the talk and the laughter: the raucous whistle of a diesel engine. In a few minutes, under the Town Bridge came the Boat-train which by chance was half-an-hour early that night. It moved very slowly along the track, as it always did, in case the line was blocked by anything. The train was led by a flagman on foot, carrying a rolled-up red flag on a stick. When he saw the large party gathered round the piano, right across the railway line, he unfurled his red flag and waved it above his head. The train came to a halt and the driver leant out of his cabin and called: 'Hey! What's going on here?'

People looked out of the train windows, peering up the quayside to discover what was holding up the train. The dragon hurried over to the man with the red flag, who was very stern and downright with him.

'Now, Sir,' he said, firmly but respectfully to the dragon, 'it seems you have a party out here, but it's against –'

His words were interrupted by a new tune on the piano, a dance tune hammered out so loudly that it quite drowned Red Flag's last words. Looking round, the dragon saw Lil seated at the piano instead of William, playing away like mad, her frizzy curls dancing round her head, and many of the people forming couples and weaving round the piano in time to the music.

The dragon turned away from this cheerful scene to find Red Flag trying to speak to him again. The dragon graciously inclined an ear and the railway official spoke loudly and slowly into it:

'This here party, Sir, all this dancing over the track – it's strictly against railway bye-laws. They got to disperse, see?'

'You mean I've got to pay you some money?' asked the dragon, feeling in his ear for his purse.

'No!' bawled Red Flag. 'Just clear them crowds off the line – disperse 'em – push 'em back, and – oh, Lord! Is that a piano I see right across the track?'

'It certainly is,' answered the dragon. 'It's the piano out of the Jolly Sailor bar, and seated at it, tickling the ivories in a most spirited manner, is Lil, the pubkeeper's lady.'

With this, the dragon folded his forepaws over his chest and stood defiantly barring the way towards the piano.

'Lil!' exclaimed Red Flag. 'Lil and me is old friends, but she ought to know better than –'

He pushed past the dragon and in a moment Lil had jumped up from the piano stool and advanced towards him, calling out:

'Jim! Jim Maitland! Come on over and join in. It's a wonderful party.'

Red Flag frowned, and pointing his flag at the piano,

he ordered Lil to get the instrument moved off the line, or he'd call the police.

'Don't be a spoilsport, Jim,' pleaded Lil. 'It's a special party for the dragon. It'll never happen again.'

'Not for centuries,' put in the dragon.

'That dragon!' exclaimed Red Flag. 'He's turning Weymouth upside down. I'll dragon him!'

And with that, Jim Maitland marched up to the dragon, looking as if he was about to knock him down with his flagstick.

'Never say die!' screamed Jacko, suddenly waking up under his green baize cover which the dragon had slipped over his cage for fear he caught cold in the evening air.

The dragon gave a wide, wide grin as he watched Red Flag, whose hand was, truth to tell, shaking as he waved it angrily at the dragon, crying:

'G-g-get your p-p-party off the track!'

But the next moment, Red Flag was swept aside by five or six passengers who had leapt out of their carriages and were hurrying to take part in the dancing themselves. Lil struck a tremendous chord and launched into the waltz *Gold and Silver*.

More passengers came pouring out of the train. They formed couples and joined in the waltz. Even the engine-driver climbed down from his cab and grabbed a buxom lady round the waist and started dancing down the quay with her. Fred was swinging young Laura round, while William had Daisy clasped to his chest. The two boys found partners, and Jeff was whirling round with an excited teenager in his arms. Denis, Hugh and Jean were doing a kind of threesome and almost collapsing with laughter.

Red Flag and Dragon surveyed the scene.

'Wonderful, isn't it?' said the dragon. 'I've never seen such a party. Not even in King Arthur's day. My party – no, no, Weymouth harbour's own party. Come on! Join in!'

He seized Red Flag's hand in his hot paw and half dragged him towards the dancing throng.

'Hullo!' cried one of the women who was standing near the pub watching the goings-on. 'Hullo! If it isn't my cousin Jim! Well, I never! Come on, Jim! Give me a whirl!'

And Jim found himself dancing like the rest. His red flag dropped to the ground. The dragon at once picked it up and stuck it behind his ear. Then he bowed politely to an elderly lady and said: 'Madam, I can't dance easily because of my tail, but I could waltz you round, if you'd care to honour me.'

'Oh, my goodness!' exclaimed the lady, and turning to her husband she said: 'See, Henry, here's someone who don't think me too old to dance!'

The dragon took her hand and turned her round like a top, handing her from paw to paw, under and over, until she was quite breathless and asked him to stop. At

that moment, the Channel Boat-train hooted several times. The dancers stopped. Lil rose from the piano. William and Fred and a few other men pushed the piano quickly off the line and the passengers, breathless and happy, hurried back to the train and scrambled into their compartments. The engine-driver started up the diesel and gave three hoarse toots on his whistle; he couldn't move, however, until he could see Red Flag walking in front of the engine. But the unfortunate flagman, Jim Maitland, was searching everywhere for his red flag. At last, with his face as red as his missing flag, he gave up the search and walked slowly along the line, the train following him. The passengers waved and cheered and the crowd outside the Jolly Sailor cheered and waved back.

The Boat-train disappeared at last, and the party began to break up with much good humour and laughter. Sybil stalked about, her tail in the air, and finally departed towards the Mary-Rose Café with a large escort of people who wanted cups of tea or coffee. The dragon, Fred and William, stood by the piano, with Lil beside them, calling out goodnights to everyone. It was Lil who first saw the red flag wound round its stick.

'Why, Dragon!' she cried. 'You've got Jim's red flag stuck behind your ear!'

The dragon blushed a little. 'I know,' he said. 'I hope he won't get into trouble for losing it. I took rather a fancy to it, to tell the truth. I'm going to take it back to Cornwall and it will decorate my cave as long as I live.'

11

Thief! Thief!

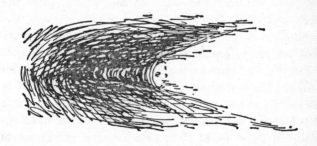

THE goodbyes were said under a deep blue sky, studded with stars. Above the roofs of the harbour houses on the opposite quay hung a full moon, as yellow as the dragon's horns. Adam and John were sleepy, and soon disappeared down the quay towards their boarding-house. John turned back to call out:

'Old dragon! Thanks for a super party!'

The dragon blew him a green smoke-ring. Then he said goodbye to Fred and William, the Leaners and Daisy and Mr and Mrs Jackson of the Jolly Sailor Inn. It was time for sleep, and a rather weary dragon began to make a slow progress down some stone steps into the water, the tide being then fairly low. Jeff followed him.

'What happened to Maurice?' asked the dragon, as Jeff walked gently over the HIS mat that he'd spread over his back, to reach *Money-Spider*.

'He wasn't feeling too good. He stayed on board,' replied Jeff. "Night, dragon, sleep well!'

The harbour settled down for the night. Only the shouts and laughter of a few late-night revellers echoed across the water, reverberating from side to side, as though a ball of sound were bouncing backwards and forwards between the walls of the houses, pubs and harbour stores.

Sometimes, you can be so happy at the end of the day that you can't sleep. The dragon found that he was wide awake for at least half-an-hour after tying up to his bollard. He looked up at the brilliant stars and said to himself in a low, murmuring voice: 'How strange it is that I see the *same* stars as these when I'm down in Cornwall, all those miles away. I am not a mathematical creature. I am not scientific. I don't understand all this business of galaxies and laser-beams and light-years. I just *enjoy* the stars. I'd like to see another comet. I really would like that. If I were the first to see it, they'd name it after me: R. Dragon's Comet. Like Halley's. It would have a tail like mine, only it would be golden not green.'

The dragon sighed. He was very happy about the party, but looking up at the stars had reminded him of a night many years before, when a little girl called Sue came out of her cottage in Cornwall and sat on his sea-weed rug and looked at the stars with him. He had shown her the constellation called the Dragon. It was up there tonight, sprawling across the sky just above the winking lighthouse at the end of the stone pier.

'Either the world is very large, or England is very small,' mused the dragon, still wondering why he saw in Weymouth the same stars that he knew so well in Cornwall. Somehow, as the time passed and the harbour settled down to sleep, this starry dragon got mixed up with the fairy lights of the party, with a little girl in a nightie, with a jolly lady called Lil who had brassy curls, and with the inside of a furniture van where he, the dragon, had sat at a piano and thumped out *Rule Britannia!* while William beat time with a screwdriver, and Fred sat at the wheel driving through the green west country lanes.

He gave one more look upwards and saw that some of the stars had disappeared behind heavy clouds. Then he closed his eyes and within a few minutes his gentle snoring joined the other night sounds of the harbour – the rattle of rigging in the wind, the slap of water against boats' hulls as the tide turned, the creak of wood against wood, and the solid footsteps of a policeman walking down the quay. The policeman stopped beside the dragon and shone his torch down upon the long, green figure, with its golden fins and horns.

'Fast asleep,' murmured the policeman to himself with affection. This was his regular beat and he had grown fond of the dragon. He shone his torch down once more and muttered: 'I suppose I'll have to admit one day that I've gone barmy. A dragon in the harbour! Either I'm dreaming or I'm barmy.'

The dragon opened an angry eye. 'Please put your torch out, Constable,' he demanded. 'I *am* a dragon. You are *not* dreaming nor are you barmy. Go away and let me sleep.'

'Sorry, Dragon,' said the policeman, humbly, and went on his way.

The dragon's dreams now took him back to his cave at Constantine Bay in Cornwall. He saw again his sea-weed rugs, his sewing-machine lid (that one day would come in useful), his rock shelves and all the little things that made it home. Perhaps it was this dream that made him talk next day of going back to Cornwall soon.

John and Adam were standing on the quay the next morning after breakfast. The sky was overclouded, the water whipped into curling waves by the rising wind, and the dragon was extremely irritable. He reached for his suitcase, took out his woolly hat and put it on.

'Might catch my death in this wind,' he muttered, and then to the boys he said: 'What are you up to?'

'We're waiting for Fred,' began Adam.

'He's probably sleeping late, as I'm trying to do,' said the dragon in a growly, grumpy voice.

'Sorry if we've woken you, Dragon, but it's important. You see, Mrs Simmonds –'

'Never heard of her,' growled the dragon and shut his eyes.

'She's our landlady,' explained John, 'and we asked her –'

'Never mind,' interrupted the dragon. 'You can forget about the Daddy's Sauce now. I'm leaving shortly and anyway I'm getting sick of it.'

'Oh, Dragon, *do* listen,' pleaded Adam.

'Listen to what?'

'What we're trying to tell you,' said John.

'I've got to listen, haven't I, seeing that I've got ears? Short of stuffing them with seaweed, I'm obliged to listen to your tiresome voices. And so far all I've learnt is that your landlady is called Mrs Simpkins. Now go away.'

'Right!' said John briskly. 'It's Simmonds, incidentally, not Simpkins. Come on, Adam. He doesn't want to know.'

'O.K.,' agreed Adam. 'Where's William and Fred?

You don't think they've gone straight there, do you, John?'

'Straight where?' asked the dragon quickly.

'Where we're going,' replied Adam, grinning at the dragon's curiosity. He turned to his brother. 'I'm still sure I saw someone going into the sail-loft last night, after the party.'

'You can't have done,' retorted John. 'I've got the key here in my hand. And why should William or Fred go there without us?'

'I don't know, but it certainly did look like someone.'

'It was probably the ghost of a sailor who once kept his sails there,' suggested the dragon.

But the boys took no notice for at that moment William was seen coming down the steps from the bridge, reading a paper as he came. The dragon looked over his shoulder and watched. He was intensely curious to know what the boys were talking about, and now, to his great annoyance, he couldn't hear what they were telling William. There was much waving of arms and pointing of fingers.

'I'm left out,' thought the dragon gloomily. 'And it's all my own fault. I shouldn't have been so bad-tempered.'

The boys and William were now very near his mooring.

'Is he still asleep?' the dragon heard William ask.

'No,' answered John. 'He's really awake but very cross.'

'I'm not!' bellowed the dragon.

'I expect it's just a hangover from all that food and drink last night,' suggested John kindly.

'No it isn't,' contradicted the dragon. 'I'm wide awake and feeling very fresh and bright. Now, what are we doing this morning? Are we all going to take a walk along the quay, or the esplanade?' He began to untie his mooring rope.

'I think we ought to tell him,' said William. 'After all, we are his friends. May the garland of friendship, you know, and all that –'

'It's rude to whisper,' said the dragon very loudly.

Jacko, now thoroughly aroused, screamed: 'One, two, three, four, *can* say five but I won't!'

'O.K., let's tell him,' said John.

'Here we go again!' remarked Jacko, swinging himself upside down. 'Whoops-a-daisy!'

John began again. 'You know that William and Fred are losing their warehouse next week?'

'Never say die!' put in Jacko at exactly the same time as the dragon said: 'Losing? What d'you mean, losing? You can't lose a warehouse – leave it in a cupboard or drop it in the harbour.'

'He means that our lease is up,' explained William. 'We only had it for one year, and the Council won't give us longer. So far we haven't found anywhere suitable, until yesterday, when the boys made a very useful suggestion.'

'It's our landlady, Mrs Simmonds, really. She owns an old building behind her house, a funny-shaped place. It was an old sail-loft – the house once belonged to a sea-captain. She doesn't use it.'

'She hasn't any sails, I suppose,' said the dragon.

'That must be it,' said John. 'Well, we asked her would she let it and she said she might.'

'So we're going to look at it now,' said Adam. 'We've got the key.'

'And we'd better be getting along,' said William. 'Fred's going to meet us there at eleven o'clock. He's just been to get his hair cut first. You coming with us, Dragon?'

'I'll think about it,' said the dragon, hoping that someone would say: 'But of course you must come. We couldn't inspect a sail-loft without you, dear Dragon. We shall need your advice.'

But no one said this, and the boys and William were hurrying away from him, so he called out rather anxiously: 'I'll catch you up. I'll swim along to the steps near the Channel boats.'

The dragon slipped out between *Money-Spider* and the quay, and started to swim very fast up the harbour.

Now it happened this morning that there was no Channel boat moored at the pier. This pier, where the ferry boats took on passengers and cars, was much shorter and broader than the stone quay on the opposite side of the harbour, the one with the lighthouse on the end of it. On the pier stood the Pavilion Theatre, a big car park and some harbour offices. It was built on thick wooden piles, held together with criss-cross girders of iron.

Just as the dragon came up to the steps near the Pavilion, his eye caught a movement underneath the pier just ahead of him. He paused for a moment, and saw a man scrambling along one of the iron girders. The man hadn't seen the dragon because his back was towards him, and he was too busy climbing as quickly as he could from girder to girder, apparently making for a small dinghy tied up to one of the wooden piles. The dragon saw that he was carrying a parcel. He watched for a few minutes,

without moving. Suddenly the man turned to reach for a handhold, and saw the dragon's yellow eyes shining like searchlights into the iron girders behind him. He uttered a scream, dropped the parcel into the sea beneath him, and started to scramble away from those eyes as quickly as he could. There was no way of escape for him, for on every side and underneath him was just sea. The dinghy for which he seemed to be making was still well out of his reach.

The dragon understood the scream instantly. It meant: 'Help! I'm caught!'

'Ho! Ho!' bellowed the dragon. 'What do you think you're doing on those girders?' His voice boomed and echoed under the pier. This was frightening enough, but even more terrifying was a strong blast of green smoke that wreathed itself round the supports like a thick cloud, and half choked him. As the smoke cleared, the dragon saw the man making a last scramble towards the dinghy, but he was now nearly within reach of the dragon's claws. He gave a despairing cry, jumped into the water and started to swim across the harbour.

'Oh, no, you don't!' cried the dragon, and swam as fast as a motor launch to cut off the man's escape. Certain now who he was, the dragon snorted through the spray he was creating: 'You're Spicer! Give yourself up!'

Frightened though the man was at hearing his name shouted, and by this enormous green creature that was blowing smoke at him and glaring with eyes like yellow searchlights, he was even more afraid of drowning. He was a poor swimmer and his clothes weighed him down heavily. When the dragon held out a paw, he clung to it thankfully with both hands, and through chattering teeth, he managed to get out: 'L-l-look here, I m-m-must g-g-get out of the water. I'm half d-d-drowned. Help me across to the other side of the harbour. I'll pay you g-g-good money. Really I w-w-will.'

'Not interested in the money,' said the dragon. 'Tell me why you can't get out on *this* side of the harbour. It's much nearer, isn't it?'

'I'm d-d-dying of c-c-cold,' pleaded the man. 'P-p-please, whatever you are, just g-g-get me across. M-m-y – er – m-m-y home's over there.'

'Then what are you doing over *here*?' asked the dragon, firmly holding the man's hand in his paw, and settling down in the water for a cosy chat. 'Do tell me about· yourself,' he added.

'Let me go! I'll swim for it!' cried the fellow, desperately trying to pull his hand away, but the dragon was too quick for him. He tightened his grip and clamped his other forepaw onto the man's shoulder. There he was, held prisoner between the dragon's two muscular and scaly arms.

By this time, the dragon's behaviour, half under the pier among the girders, had attracted some attention. Harbour police, customs officers and others were standing on the edge of the quay, peering down at him. Suddenly a police car's sirens sounded very close, a car stopped with a screech of brakes, and three policemen pushed their way through the little knot of people.

'Hi, there! Dragon!' shouted one of the policemen. 'That's the fellow we want. That's Spicer! Hold him!'

'I have him as safe as if he were in a dungeon,' replied the dragon, calmly, 'but I can't stay like this forever. I shall get stiff. Send a relieving force as soon as possible.'

'There's a police launch just coming up!' called the policeman, and sure enough it came up alongside the dragon within a couple of minutes.

'Nice work, Dragon!' exclaimed one of the harbour police. 'A fair cop!'

The wretched Spicer, owner of the Spider's Web junk shop, was a bedraggled creature when the police pulled him out of the water into their launch. He kept glancing back at the dragon, as though he still couldn't believe he was not dreaming.

'Copped by a dragon!' he muttered, as the police turned their launch and began sailing down the harbour again. 'I must have had too much to drink. Copped by a dragon? It can't be true.'

'It's true enough,' said one of the policemen. 'Here, wrap this coat round you. We don't want you dying of pewmonia just yet.'

Meanwhile, the dragon had swum back to the steps and

was now climbing up them. As his green head appeared, there was a general cry of 'Here he is!' and he found himself surrounded by a small crowd of officials and other people, all exclaiming with wonder at the way he had caught Spicer. The dragon found himself the hero of the hour, but though he graciously acknowledged the compliments and congratulations, he kept looking round for Fred and William and the boys. Why were they not here, among the others on the quay?

Suddenly John pushed through the crowd.

'Well done, old Dragon!' he cried. 'You're a hero! Come on this way to the café. William and Adam and I are all having coffee there.'

The dragon felt he could do with a hot drink, not to mention a bit of a snack, so he followed John, and a place was found for him in the Mary-Rose, near the door leading to a passage. By leaving the door open, the dragon could lay his tail out along the passage and manage to sit at the table with his friends, drinking coffee and consuming buns and sandwiches. But before he began to eat – he had actually taken a sandwich, a bun and a treacle tart and put them on his plate – the dragon looked anxiously round the room. He felt that something was wrong. He nibbled the sandwich and stared round him again. Someone was missing.

Suddenly he exclaimed: 'Fred's not here! Where's Fred?'

'He won't be long,' answered William. 'Mrs Prior is doing him up. He's been knocked out.'

'*Knocked out?*' repeated the dragon. 'Who knocked him out?'

'That fellow you've been chasing underneath the pier,'

said John. 'Fred's in the back parlour, talking to the Sergeant. Mrs Prior's attending to his head. She's probably finished bandaging him up by now.'

The dragon held the remains of his sandwich in the air. Somehow he didn't want it. He put it down on his plate and asked, in a subdued voice: 'Exactly what's happened to Fred? You're hiding something from me. Why is a policeman with him? What's he supposed to have done?'

'Silly old Dragon,' said Adam, but affectionately. 'He hasn't done anything. Not anything wrong, that is. I'll tell you what happened. When John and me and William got to the sail-loft where we were to meet Fred, we couldn't see him anywhere.'

'Then I heard a groan,' put in John.

'And I knew that groan was Fred's,' went on William. 'We found him lying under the bushes at the side of the sail-loft.'

'Knocked out and covered with blood,' added Adam, who was thoroughly enjoying the story. 'He'd been attacked by that man Spicer.'

'Spicer'd been in the sail-loft,' explained John. 'I suppose he was using it as a hide-out. He came out of it to find Fred waiting outside the door.'

'And he give Fred a thump in the left eye with his fist,' said William, 'and the next thing we hear is that our old friend R. Dragon, is chasing Spicer in and out of the girders under the pier, and –'

'And he's handed that fellow Spicer to the police!' bellowed the dragon. 'That's what I did, after playing "Here we go round the mulberry bush" with him. Now where's Fred and is he all right?'

At that moment, Fred came into the tea-room from

the back of the house, and with him came Mrs Prior, who owned the Mary-Rose Café. Fred looked rather pale and wore a bandage round his head, covering his left eye.

'Lucky I took that first-aid course,' said Mrs Prior. 'Came in very handy. I been longing to do something with me first-aid kit for months.'

The dragon had scrambled up on his back legs. 'Fred!' he cried. 'Tell me everything, Fred. I'm only beginning to catch up.'

Fred sat down at the table and they passed him a cup of coffee. Sybil appeared, looked round the company and decided to sit on Fred's knee, where she could hear the whole story comfortably.

'Well,' began Fred, 'I had my hair cut, and I waited for you just outside the sail-loft like you said, and then I heard the wooden door behind me creaking and I look round, thinking it's Mrs Simmonds, perhaps, but it's not. It's this type, Spicer, and he's got a bundle wrapped up in canvas under his arm. And before I could say a word, he's knocked me down and skedaddled.'

'That's where you come in, Dragon,' said Adam. 'How did you spot Spicer?'

'I was sailing up the harbour,' said the dragon, 'intending to meet you all and help you inspect this sail-loft – thought you might like my advice, you know. But, before I climbed up the steps to the quay, I saw someone scrambling about on the girders under the pier. This seemed to me very suspicious behaviour, so I – well, I nobbled him. That's all. Nobbled him.'

The dragon reached out and nobbled a cream bun. 'How bad is your eye, Fred?' he inquired.

'It's going black,' interposed Mrs Prior. 'He hasn't

seen himself in a mirror yet, but he's all right, ain't you, Fred? And the Sergeant's told him the whole story, so you tell 'em, Fred.'

'It seems they'd been searching for this man Spicer for days. He'd left his shop – you know, the Spider's Web. He'd locked it up and the police waited for a few days and then they raided it. They'd been tipped off with some information about this Spicer, the Sergeant said, and they wanted to question him.'

'*We* saw the police going into the shop,' exclaimed Adam. 'They wouldn't say what they were looking for.'

'Well, I can tell you,' said Fred. 'They were looking for contraband. That's stuff like tobacco and whisky and brandy, but that's not all. The real money's in drugs, drugs like heroin and cannabis, and they had a tip-off from someone that Spicer was using the shop as cover-up for a bit of drug-smuggling.'

'He had a parcel with him,' said the dragon. 'He dropped it into the water just before I caught him.'

'You'll have to tell the police about that,' said John.

'I shall certainly tell the police,' said the dragon. 'No doubt a detective will soon be asking for my advice and assistance.'

'Was this chap Spicer a fence?' asked Adam.

'That's what he was,' answered Fred.

'A kind of go-between,' explained William. 'He was buying and selling contraband and stolen goods in a small way. Doing it for years, apparently, but they'd never caught him. The drugs is something new, the Sergeant said.'

'We've known him since we came to Weymouth,' said Fred. 'We thought he might have a small line in fiddling, as you might say, but it was nothing to do with us. William and me's taken one or two things to London for him in our van. He always paid on the nail, and of course we don't ask questions. All his parcels were very securely tied up. Nothing really important, I daresay.'

There was a short silence. The dragon was worried. He'd suspected that Maurice and Jeff might have contraband aboard the *Money-Spider*, but *drugs*? Could these young men have got themselves mixed up with drug-smuggling? Was this why they were so anxious and short-tempered when they found the Spider's Web shut, day after day? The dragon liked Maurice and Jeff. They had become his friends, and his suspicions made him very unhappy.

'Have another sandwich?' he asked, to break the silence. He picked up the plate and waved it about vaguely.

'No, thanks,' said Fred, absently taking one all the same.

'Anyone else?' asked the dragon.

'You eat it, Dragon,' suggested John.

'Actually there are *two* left,' said the dragon and then wondered why he'd said it. He didn't feel hungry.

'You eat 'em both,' said William.

Again there was silence. The dragon still held the plate but he did not eat the sandwiches. He was thinking how

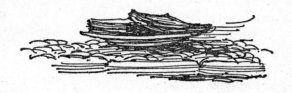

puzzled he'd been at first when they talked about being 'loaded' and having to 'unload' the yacht. Now he knew what they meant and he didn't like it at all.

At last Fred said: 'I think we'd best be going along to see Mrs Simmonds about renting her sail-loft. After all, that's what we set out to do this morning, and we do need it. We've got to get our stuff out of the Council's warehouse by Monday morning.'

'You coming with us, Dragon?' asked William.

'You know we'd like to have your advice,' put in Fred.

The dragon looked thoughtful.

'No,' he said at last. 'I think there's something else I've got to do first. I'll see your sail-loft later.'

12

Goodbye Weymouth Harbour!

WHEN they all came out on the quay, the sky was completely clouded over. The wind was much stronger and blowing from the south-west, where black rain-clouds hung over the distant hills. As the dragon walked slowly down the quay, his forepaws clasped behind his back, he felt the rain beginning to fall. The quay was deserted. The Leaners had disappeared. Suddenly the dragon saw a familiar figure approaching him. It was Jeff. He was wearing only a shirt and trousers, and already the rain had darkened the blue shoulders of his shirt.

'Dragon!' he exclaimed. 'I was coming looking for you. I want to see you – urgently.'

'I want to see *you* urgently,' said the dragon. 'And I think we'd better stay out here, rain or no rain. There's no one about to overhear what we say.'

'I don't care how wet I get,' agreed Jeff, looking very miserable. 'This is a serious business.'

The dragon stood waiting, with the rain running down his scales in a most uncomfortable and tickly manner.

'Why don't you tell me the whole story?' he said at last to the unhappy Jeff, who was beginning to look rather like a bedraggled duck.

'O.K.,' said the young man at last. 'I think it's the only thing to do. You see, it's like this. *Money-Spider* belongs to Maurice's brother, Peter, who works in Paris. He's had the inside of the boat specially fitted up to take stuff – that is – well, brandy and tobacco.'

'Contraband – no duty paid on it, I suppose?'

'That's about it,' admitted Jeff. 'We often sail the boat over from France and get rid of the stuff for him. We get a small share of the profit –'

'Small?' commented the dragon. 'It seems to me you ought to get the lion's share, since you're taking all the risks.'

'Oh, well, it was fun at first,' said Jeff. 'You know – rather exciting. And then we had *Money-Spider* for sailing and a bit of racing and so on.'

'And you got rid of the stuff to our friend Spicer at the Spider's Web, that was it, I suppose?' said the dragon, shaking the rain off his ears and horns.

'That was it. But this time the wretched shop was shut, and there we were – stuck with the stuff.'

'Very awkward for you,' observed the dragon. 'Quite a tight spot.'

Jeff was silent for a moment and then he said: 'You know I told you Maurice wasn't well last night and that's why he didn't come to the party?'

The dragon nodded.

'Well, it wasn't true,' admitted Jeff gloomily.

'Oh,' said the dragon. 'In my experience – which goes back for several hundred years, of course – lies are generally a mistake. What *was* he doing?'

'He'd seen Spicer during the afternoon, seen him actually in the dinghy which he was rowing up to the pier.'

'Aha!' cried the dragon. 'The dinghy! Yes, Spicer tried to reach it when I caught him.'

'He's caught?' exclaimed Jeff.

'He is, indeed. I nobbled him,' said the dragon. 'I nobbled him this morning. He's with the police this very moment, helping them with their inquiries, as they always say. What they really mean is that they've got him just where they want him.'

'Oh, Lord!' groaned Jeff. 'I'd better get back to Maurice quickly.'

'No, you don't,' said the dragon firmly, placing a sodden paw on Jeff's already soaking shoulder. 'If you want me to help you – which I think you do – you've got to tell me the whole story, not just a bit of it.'

'Fair enough,' agreed Jeff. 'When Maurice saw Spicer in the afternoon, he made an appointment to see him yesterday night, while the party was going on. They met in a pub down by the Backwater, and Spicer told Maurice he wasn't interested in our stuff any more. He'd got onto something that brought him in a lot of money. Maurice asked him if it was drugs, and Spicer just laughed and said, "What if it is? It's nothing to do with you." Maurice said he'd go to the police, and Spicer said, "O.K., you go to the police. You got no proof in the first place, and secondly, you'll land yourself in trouble for all this stuff you've been bringing over from France. I've got friends,"

167

Spicer said, "who'd lay information about you to the police if I raised my finger." And he went on, saying, "We're in this together, chum, aren't we? I can always say you were supplying me with cannabis, can't I?" Maurice tried to threaten him, but he just laughed, and said he wasn't interested in our type of smuggling, and he warned Maurice again about his friends, and said if he split to the police or anyone else, he might find himself in the harbour in a concrete overcoat.'

'A concrete overcoat?' exclaimed the dragon. 'What on earth did he mean?'

'It's pretty nasty,' said the unhappy Jeff. 'It means – it means you kill someone and weigh them down with lumps of concrete and throw them into, say, a river or the sea. That's what he meant his friends might do to Maurice.'

'How extremely unpleasant,' said the dragon, and went quite pale green all over. 'And how very wicked as well. I think we ought to get back to *Money-Spider* and talk to Maurice as soon as possible. Both of us are soaked and might well die of pneumonia before we see him if we don't hurry.'

So they both began to walk quickly down the quay. Jeff told the dragon that Maurice was planning to get away from Weymouth after his talk with Spicer, but the tide wouldn't be right till about three that afternoon.

'Where's he planning to go?' asked the dragon.

'To Portsmouth, I think,' said Jeff. 'To try and unload the stuff there. It's brandy mostly. Brandy and a bit of tobacco.'

'Really,' said the dragon, pausing and turning to look

Jeff straight in the face. 'I never knew such a foolish pair of fellows as you two, not since my days at the court of King Arthur. A pair of idiots, that's what you are.'

'I know,' groaned Jeff.

Before either of them could say anything more, they heard a crash and shouts coming from further down the harbour, near the Town Bridge. The wind had whipped up the water into sizeable waves, and the rain was lashing down more furiously than ever. In the middle of the harbour just ahead of them a yacht was rolling about. Her sails were partly hauled up and flapping wildly in the wind, and, as they came near her, they could hear a voice shouting: 'For heaven's sake, rev up the engine, Maud! The sail's caught in the rigging! I'll have to pull it down again. I told you we oughtn't to try and get out this morning.'

The dragon recognized the voice at once – Colonel Ocklestone's. The Colonel was on deck, fighting with the mainsail, while his wife was at the tiller, trying to steer the boat and at the same time attempting to manage the engine, which she didn't understand in the least. In fact, a moment later, she pulled the throttle the wrong way and instead of revving up the engine, she simply made it putter and come to a dead stop. The yacht *Furious* was now at the mercy of the wind.

The Colonel's wife shrieked: 'I can't see where I'm going, Percy! Do get that sail down!'

'You're right across the harbour!' shouted the dragon. 'You'll hit something in a minute. Never mind the engine – try and steer her!'

Colonel Ocklestone's red face and white whiskers

peered out from the sail, which had somehow wound itself round his head and shoulders, making him look rather like an angry desert sheikh.

'Put her hard over to starboard!' shouted the Colonel to his wife, at which the poor woman, who never could remember her right hand from her left, put the tiller hard down to port. The boat, caught in the wind, sped across the harbour and hit *Money-Spider* with a resounding crash plumb amidships.

Colonel Ocklestone swore, and at last getting himself free of the flapping mainsail, turned to shout at his unfortunate wife. She, however, was not to be seen, for she had fallen over backwards into the water when the yacht hit *Money-Spider*, and before the Colonel could see her surfacing behind the boat, Maurice was up on deck, and the two men were shouting at each other in a fury.

At this point, the dragon drew level with them, and puffing out a cloud of green smoke which had the two of them choking and quite unable to go on quarrelling, he cried: 'Now then! Quarrelling won't help anyone. Maurice, is your boat watertight? Colonel, go to the stern and help your wife aboard or she'll drown.'

'Confound it!' exploded the Colonel. 'The woman doesn't know what she's doing. I was too tied up in this dashed sail to see what was happening.'

'Help! Help!' came his wife's watery voice.

'All right, all right, Maud! I'm coming!'

But the dragon was already in the water, and in a couple of shakes, he was holding out a paw to Mrs Ocklestone. He then swam up to the yacht *Furious*, and helped her aboard from behind, while the Colonel pulled her up by the arms.

'Now back you go and get on your mooring before you do any more damage!' ordered the dragon, giving the yacht a mighty thrust with his powerful forepaws, which sent it spinning across the harbour to the opposite quay.

The dragon then turned back to *Money-Spider* to see what harm had been done. Both the young men were on deck, hardly able to keep on their feet, the yacht was rocking so much. The *Furious* had cut a sizeable hole in her amidships, but fortunately not below the waterline, so that very little water was being shipped. On the other hand, *something* was undoubtedly spilling from the hole. The dragon lifted his nose and sniffed.

'Brandy!' he exclaimed.

Maurice began to deny it, but Jeff turned on him quickly and said: 'Shut up, Maurice! I've told the dragon about our cargo. It's not only the boat that's holed. We're in a hole ourselves, I can tell you."

'That's a nasty crack in your hull,' observed the dragon.

'You're telling me,' said Maurice grimly. Then he turned to Jeff and said with urgency: 'Look, the harbour police will be here at any moment because of this accident, and they'll find the – the brandy and stuff, and then we'll be done for. Come on, Jeff! Let's chuck it into the harbour.'

'Don't be such a fool,' interrupted the dragon, rocking backwards and forwards in the rough water at the side of *Money-Spider*, with one paw firmly placed on the gunwale. 'That's exactly what you *oughtn't* to do. How many bottles got smashed – roughly?'

'I don't rightly know,' answered Maurice. 'Not many. There's enough left to send us to jail, I'd say. Not to mention the tobacco. I see now what an idiot I've been.'

'You have indeed,' said the dragon crisply. 'But then, as we used to say in King Arthur's court, it's no use crying over spilt gravy. I think I can see the police launch coming down the harbour. Now listen to me. The police are very pleased with me because I caught this fellow Spicer for them. I intend to tell them that you've got this brandy and tobacco –'

'Oh, Lord!' groaned Maurice, almost in tears. 'You won't do that, will you?'

'If only you'd listen,' said the dragon, giving *Money-Spider* a shake with his paw which almost flung the two young men into the water. 'LISTEN. There isn't much time and I shall be seasick if I have to stay here much longer, rocking up and down. I *shall* tell them, and I'll say that you are going to declare the stuff to the Customs and pay the duty on it –'

'We haven't any money.'

'WILL YOU LISTEN!' roared the dragon. 'I will go bail for you. I'll say that you are both young and silly – don't protest. You are. Very young and very silly. Here they come. You and Jeff go below, Maurice, and wait till you're called up on deck.'

The dragon then swam quickly towards the harbour police-launch. At first, of course, the police were only interested in the accident itself, but the dragon knew that as soon as they went aboard *Money-Spider* to inspect the damage, they would smell the brandy, and the whole story would come out. So the first thing he said to the police was this:

'I saw the whole thing. It was no one's fault. Colonel Ocklestone and his lady –'

'Oh, them!' groaned one of the policemen.

'They got into a bit of difficulty,' went on the dragon. 'The Colonel was a bit mixed up with the mainsail, I'm afraid –'

'We can imagine,' said the other policeman. 'Now let's look at the damage.'

'Just a minute,' said the dragon. 'Don't be too hard on the Colonel. Why don't we just blame the weather?'

'Never mind the weather. Let's have a look at *Money-Spider*,' said the officer at the tiller and, revving up his engine, he tried to steer round the dragon, but the dragon was long enough to stretch almost across the harbour if he chose to. And he did.

'Dragon,' said the policeman sternly. 'You are obstructing us in our duty.'

'Not really,' answered the dragon calmly. 'I just had things I wanted to say.'

'They must wait.'

'They can't wait. And anyway, who caught Spicer for you?'

'Well, of course you did, Dragon. Now let us sail round you, please.'

'Just make me a promise,' said the dragon, without moving, and putting both forepaws on the gunwale of the launch, so that it leant over towards him.

'What promise?' said the policeman, a little impatiently.

'You'll smell brandy when you get aboard *Money-Spider*.'

'Oh, shall we? And has it been declared?'

'Not yet,' replied the dragon, giving the launch a bit of a rock.

'In that case it's contraband. The Customs men will confiscate it and that mightn't be the end of the matter. Your young friends may find themselves in big trouble. Will you stop rocking this boat and –'

'You haven't made your promise,' said the dragon, slowly waving his tail which almost touched the opposite quay. 'I'll undertake to see that duty is paid on the contraband stuff these lads have. It belongs to someone else, to Maurice's brother, in fact, and I'm going to have something to say to him.'

'That's not the point,' said the policeman patiently. 'If they've got contraband aboard, and not declared it –'

The dragon shook the launch again, saying: 'Remember how I caught Spicer for you? Well then. Promise me you'll say nothing to the Customs about the brandy and tobacco. I'm making you a promise that the duty will be paid. That's one promise in exchange for another.'

The two policemen in the launch looked at each other.

'All right,' agreed the man at the helm. 'That is, we *shall* report it in the course of our duty, but you'll have time to carry out *your* promise first. After that, it's not our business anyway. If Customs make them pay a fine, it's up to them.'

'Thank you,' said the dragon. '*Noblesse oblige*, as we used to say in King Arthur's court.'

'We're not in King Arthur's court now,' said the second policeman rather sourly.

'Well, don't you wish you were?' said the dragon with a beaming smile, as he swam out of their way.

While the harbour police were examining the damage on *Money-Spider*, the dragon quickly crossed the harbour and talked to Colonel Ocklestone. He was in a state of

much agitation at the damage his boat had done to
Money-Spider. He cheered up a little when the dragon
told him that he had assured the harbour police that he
himself had witnessed the accident, and felt that the
weather was more to blame than anything else.

'Pity about the boys' boat, though,' said the Colonel
ruefully. 'Done some damage, I'm afraid. Of course, the
insurance will take care of it, but it's put them out of
racing or even sailing. I feel very bad about it.'

'You needn't feel too bad,' said the dragon. 'The
weather will probably put a stop to racing anyway, and
Maurice and Jeff have other worries.'

The dragon had decided that the Colonel was not a bad
old fellow, and that it might be worth confiding to him
exactly what those worries were. Nothing venture,
nothing have, muttered the dragon to himself, as he had
done once before in Weymouth harbour. People are
usually nicer than you think, he went on to say to
himself. So he told the Colonel the story of the brandy
and tobacco, and Maurice's brother Peter.

The Colonel blew out his white whiskers like a frill
and said: 'Most distressed to hear about this. Most distressed. I wouldn't want to be the cause of those lads
being caught. Of course it's contraband, and against the
law, but they're only young shavers. Dammit, I remember coming back from France when I was a subaltern,
with a dozen bottles of brandy for the Officer's Mess and
a diamond-studded watch for the little wife. Boys will be
boys, y'know.'

'Yes, they will be,' agreed the dragon. 'You could be
a help, Colonel.'

'Me? How?'

'Well, they're turning the stuff into the Customs, and making a clean breast of it. If they're lucky, they'll just have to pay the duty. And the Customs people will confiscate it all, of course. But they may also fine them. I believe the fine can be quite heavy, and those boys haven't any money.'

'Dear, dear,' muttered the Colonel. 'Bad luck. Very bad luck. All my fault that they've been found out, eh?'

'Well, partly,' said the dragon, for he knew that they would have been found out anyway. Spicer would have told the police about his dealings with Maurice and Jeff in the past.

The old Colonel rubbed his rain-soaked whiskers, and said at last: 'Well, we're all young once. And we all do damn silly things sometimes. But I like those two boys. Suppose I offer to pay the fine for 'em, if they *are* fined?'

'Your hand, Colonel!' cried the dragon. 'I knew you would!' and he clasped the Colonel's large red hand in his own damp green paw.

The Customs officers confiscated all that was left of the brandy and tobacco, and fined the two young men two hundred pounds. Colonel Ocklestone was as good as his word. He paid the fine, and a contrite and subdued Maurice and Jeff swore that they would never engage in smuggling again.

The gale blew itself out and on a fine, sunny morning, about a week after the party, Maurice and Jeff said goodbye to the dragon. Their boat was in dock being repaired, and they were going back to London by train.

'And I'm off, too. Back to Constantine Bay,' said the

dragon. 'I've sent on all my luggage. I'll have to tie Jacko's cage onto my back. I'm not sure how.'

'I'd ask the Leaners,' suggested Jeff. 'They're old sailors and know how these things are done. They're wizards with knots.'

So, after seeing Maurice and Jeff off on the train, the dragon went back to the quay and talked to the Leaners about his problem. Bill and George at once produced some tarry twine and, very expertly, they tied the cage to the dragon's back, and wrapped some tarpaulin round it to prevent Jacko getting wet on the journey. They left the top open so that he had air and could see out if he clung to the top of the cage, and they left a flap of tarpaulin that could be pulled right over the cage at night or if it rained. Quite a crowd gathered on the quay to see this interesting operation, and everyone exclaimed what a wonderful, seamanlike job Bill Pouncy and George Snook had done. Sailor Pearce, who had sold Jacko to the dragon, came over from Portland to say goodbye, and was heard to declare that he couldn't have made a better job of the knots himself. He looked very dashing with his blue fisherman's smock, his curly hair, brown face, and peaked cap with a piece of sea-thrift stuck in it. This he took out and tucked behind the dragon's ear – to remind him of Weymouth, he said.

Jacko meanwhile was giving a great farewell performance of his favourite sayings: 'Whoops-a-daisy! Never say die! Here we go again!' And finally, peering out at the crowd from his position upside down at the top of his cage, he shrieked: 'One, two, three, four, can say FIVE but I won't!'

William and Fred were there, of course, and promised that the next time they had any goods to transport to or from Cornwall, they'd drive the van themselves and come to Constantine Bay to see the dragon.

Adam and John were going home, too, and both shook the dragon's paw and said they'd never forget him. Lil pushed them all aside to give the dragon a huge parcel of sandwiches for the journey and a smacking kiss on his scaly cheek.

'Well,' said the dragon at last, with a sigh, 'I suppose I must be off.'

For a moment he felt very sad, leaving so many good friends. Even the Yacht Club Secretary was there to see him off, and the Harbour-Master too, with his Assistant, Mr Tanner. In their different ways, all these people had helped to add up to the word 'Weymouth', which the dragon had come to love.

The Leaners were the last to shake his paw. Both were looking very mysterious about something, winking at each other, nudging their elbows into people's ribs, their brown, wrinkled faces creased into smiles.

'We got a secret for you, Dragon,' they said. 'Just you wait a minute. You mustn't start leaving the harbour till *it* arrives.'

'Till what arrives?' asked the dragon.

Everyone burst out laughing but in a very nice way. It seemed that he was the only one who didn't know the joke. Then suddenly: 'Here they are!' shouted the crowd, and onto the quay came marching the Weymouth Town Silver Band, in their smart uniforms.

'Goodbye, Dragon!' people cried. 'Have a good

journey! Come back and see us again! Goodbye! Goodbye!'

The dragon waved a paw in farewell and blew some green smoke-rings over the heads of the crowd. Then he started swimming up the harbour towards the open sea, and as he left the quayside the Weymouth Town Silver Band struck up with *It's a long way to Tipperary*, the song that William and the dragon had sung in the furniture van once upon a time, and that the dragon himself had sung, to slightly different words, as he walked up the quay after fetching his luggage.

The dragon turned his head and looked back as he approached the mouth of the harbour. There was the Town Silver Band still playing, and the people waving and singing, and in front of the crowd, a very small figure – Sybil, the mackerel-coloured cat from the Mary-Rose Café.

'Here we go!' shrieked Jacko from behind the dragon's ears, and then he whistled melodiously above the sound of the sea.

The dragon turned his head and looked back to see two figures pounding down the stone quay, which he was just passing on his way out to the open sea. They were John and Adam.

'*Bon voyage!*' shouted John. 'That's French – it means have a good journey!'

'I say! I say!' panted Adam. 'How many dragons' tails would it take to reach the moon?'

'I can guess that one!' the dragon shouted back. 'One, if it's long enough!'

The sound of the Silver Band could no longer be heard.

The figures of the two boys became tiny. The dragon was out in Weymouth Bay, the stone quay getting smaller and smaller behind him. He gave a great puff of green smoke that was quickly carried away on the wind. He turned westwards and as he swam round the Isle of Portland, he could hear Jacko quietly whistling to himself a few snatches of the tune of *Tipperary*.

'Funny old Jacko,' murmured the dragon. 'It'll be good to have you living in my cave in Constantine Bay. It'll be like having a piece of Weymouth always with me.'

Were you ever on Weymouth quay?

Oh, say were you ev-er on Wey-mouth quay? Oh___ Wey-mouth! It's there that the ri-ver runs down to the sea, And I'm bound for Wey-mouth quay. So it's heave up___ my bag, Way___ down Wey-mouth___ Up with my lug-gage and up with my cage, And I'm bound,___ for Wey-mouth quay!___

It's a long, long way to Weymouth harbour

(With grateful thanks to 'It's a long, long way to
Tipperary' for the tune and the basis of the words.)

It's a long way___ to Wey-mouth har-bour,
___ It's a long way___ to go!___ It's a
long way___ to Wey-mouth har-bour,___ And the
ni-cest pub I know!___ And William's
___ at the pia-no,___ And Fred is keep-ing time,
___ It's a long, long way to Wey-mouth har -
-bour, And I can't think of ano-ther rhyme!

© 1912 Reproduced by kind permission of B. Feldman & Co. Ltd
138-140 Charing Cross Road, London, WC2H OLD

Old R. Dragon had a ride

Old R. Dra-gon had a ride In Fred 'nd William's

van-o! And on that ride he sang some songs,

In Fred 'nd Will–iam's van-o! With a

toot toot here, And a honk honk there,

Here a toot, there a toot, Here and there a honk honk!

Old R. Dra-gon had a ride, E–I–E–I–O!

Billy boy

Can she cook a bit o' steak Bil-ly boy, Bil-ly boy? Can she cook a bit o' steak, me Bil-ly boy? She can cook a bit o' steak, Aye, and make a gird-le cake, And me Nan-cy kit-tled me fan-cy, Oh, me charm-ing Bil-ly boy!

KEPT IN THE DARK
Nina Bawden

Clara and Bosie and Noel all found the big strange isolated house and the grandparents they'd never met before rather daunting. And when David turned up and claimed he belonged there too, things got even more disturbing. There were so many secrets to find the answers to.

THE CLOCK TOWER GHOST
Gene Kemp

Addlesbury Tower is haunted by Rich King Cole, a mean old man who fell off it long ago in mysterious circumstances. Its newest terror is Mandy – feared by her family and eventually by the ghost too. In the war they wage to dominate the tower, Mandy and King Cole do frightful and funny things to each other, little guessing how much they really have in common.

JEFFY, THE BURGLAR'S CAT

Ursula Moray Williams

Nobody who saw Miss Amity and her cat Jeffy walking to the shops each day would have believed that the old lady was a burglar. Only Jeffy knew the terrible truth and was determined to reform his wicked mistress. But all his efforts to prevent Miss Amity from back-sliding were foiled when she took in a stray kitten, Little Lew, who turned out to be the perfect partner in crime . . .

DOG DAYS AND CAT NAPS

Gene Kemp

Ten stories about animals – and their human owners. Cats and dogs are particularly prominent, but mice, gerbils and other assorted animals also weave their way through this delightfully funny and off-beat collection.

UP WITH SKOOL!

Crammed with jokes, puns and limericks sent in by children from all over the country, *Up with Skool!* shows you the funny side of the place you either love or hate. And ten star personalities contribute their own funny stories of school: Harry Secombe on cricket, Roald Dahl on punishment, Cyril Smith MP on school dinners, etc. Who says school's a bad joke?

THE FOX BUSTERS

· *Dick King-Smith*

The chickens of Foxearth Farm were a very special lot – they had long legs, were quick witted, but most important of all, they could fly! They really could fly – up and away out of the reach of foxes. The Foxearth Fowl found their names on bits of writing scattered about the farm, like Fisons, and Leyland and Trespassers and Beware Of. And one day Massey-Harris became the father of three chicks so exceptional that they were given brand-new names, for Ransome, Sims and Jefferies could fly faster, higher and further than any before them. And when a group of determined young foxes kept laying plans for one fiendishly cunning raid after another, the legendary three found a way of outwitting the most crafty of them. Not for nothing would they one day be known as The Fox Busters!

CARBONEL AND CALIDOR

Babara Sleigh

'You do look a Charlie!' said John, when Rosemary tried on the
paper hat, but Rosemary didn't feel like laughing. She felt strangely
solemn. Then she tried on the ring which had fallen from the
cracker, and she thought she heard a voice say, 'Help, John and
Rosemary.' It was only later that she discovered their old friend
Carbonel, King of the Fallowhithe cats, needed their help to search
for his runaway son, Prince Calidor, and that the flashing red ring
had turned her and John into Hearing Humans, who could understand the language of animals.

MORE TELEVISION ADVENTURES OF
WORZEL GUMMIDGE

Keith Waterhouse & Willis Hall

Admirers of Worzel Gummidge will know by now that keeping
the crows away from Ten-acre Field will never keep him out of
trouble. In fact, there is no end to the predicaments he can get
into, such as turning up at school in his Thinking Head and
astonishing the staff with his great brain, or stowing away in a
charabanc during the old people's outing, and being pursued by
Saucy Nancy, who had spent most of her career as a ship's
figurehead.

But the most important thing in Worzel's life is his devotion to
that stiff-jointed little creature, Aunt Sally, however disdainfully
she might treat him. And for her he even puts on his Gardening
Head and tries to do an honest bit of work.

These new stories about Worzel have been created for television
by the authors of the first collection, *The Television Adventures of
Worzel Gummidge*.

THE CARTOONIST
Betsy Byars

Alfie dashed up to his attic to draw funny cartoons at every possible moment. Life, as Alfie saw it, was in those cartoons, and they were a secret world more precious to him than the one around him. When his family tried to take over the attic, Alfie barricaded himself in, determined to sit it out . . .

THE SNOW HOUSE
Nora Wilkinson

If a deputation of excessively nice and polite mice told you they were in danger of starvation and death from fearful traps, wouldn't you want to help? Well, Fred certainly did, and he invited them to go and live in the Snow House (an enormous snowball) which was just the right size for them. There were difficulties, of course, and the actual journey across the snowy Square at midnight was fraught with peril. But eventually they were all safely installed and living happily, until something even worse happened – they were kidnapped, and seemed destined for a fate worse than death. This is the story of the biggest and most daring rescue in Mouse History, and it will be enjoyed by everyone who feels friendly towards mice.

KING DEATH'S GARDEN
Ann Halam

Maurice has discovered a way of visiting the past, and whatever its dangers it's too exciting for him to want to give up – yet. A subtle and intriguing ghost story for older readers.

STRAW FIRE
Angela Hassall

Kevin and Sam meet Mark, an older boy who is sleeping rough up on the Heath behind their street. Kevin feels there is something weird about Mark, something he can't quite put his finger on. And he is soon to discover that there is something very frightening and dangerous about Mark too.